Soggy Saturday Sandwich

By
Stuart Reid

Illustrations, Cover and Layouts
By John Pender

Gorgeous Garage Publishing Ltd
Falkirk, Scotland

Copyright ©2022 Stuart Reid

The rights of Stuart Reid to be identified as the author of this work and the full Gorgeous George series, under the Copyright, Designs and Patents Act 1988, has been asserted by him.

Cover design and illustrations by John Pender
Cover and illustrations copyright
© Gorgeous Garage Publishing Ltd

Photographs used by kind permission of
Betty Logan and John Pender

First Edition
This edition published in the UK by
Gorgeous Garage Publishing Ltd
ISBN : 978-1-910614-16-7

Mums, dads and teachers can follow Stuart on Twitter:

@StuartReidBooks

DEDICATION

To the pupils and staff at Kinloss Primary
School, Kinloss, Mrs Wolford, Carlene and all
the brilliant teachers.

Thank you for looking after me at every visit over
the years, especially that icy, snowy day!

And for Johnny-boy…

My bestest-ever best mate, my pal and
my buddy for over 35 years. We started in the
supermarket together, and you'll know some of
these storylines. You'll also recognise one or two
characters, and certainly remember the trolleys,
the shouting and the cauliflowers!

Thanks, pal.

. . . .

*For my wife Angela and my little boy Lucas,
whose love, encouragement and unrelenting
patience means the absolute world to me.*

*Thank you for letting daddy
live out his drawing dream!*

Love always, John xXx

SOGGY SATURDAY SANDWICH

CONTENTS

Introduction

By popular request, this book has Yuck Alert warnings at the start of certain chapters, for anyone who is a little bit delicate about yucky stuff, (mainly mums and dads and teachers). You know, words like *bum, poo* and *bottom burps*. Not all the chapters are yucky but you'll find that out soon enough.

Oh, and this chapter of the book was meant to be called **The Prologue** but there is a rumour that some people skip past the prologue. Even teachers! So, it has been called **Introduction**, which is a bit boring but blame those cheeky chapter skippers.

Prologues shouldn't really be missed out because authors use them for various purposes, often setting the scene, hinting at problems that the heroes of each story might face, or to give readers extra information that advances the plot. In this case, mainly, it is used to tell the readers (that's you) a little bit about two of the main characters, George and Kenny.

Okay so far? Good. So, let's get started.

Friends. Buddies. BFF's. Call it what you want but these two lads were close, like two crossed-fingers-tight close.

Gorgeous George and Crayon Kenny had spent long summer months and school holidays fighting aliens, chasing Loch Ness monsters and being chased by snot zombies. They fought pirates, a leprechaun and had even watched a man splat his head all the way up into an elephant's bottom. Their summer-time struggles had bonded them together into the best of buddies.

George and Kenny laughed at each other's jokes. They laughed at their own jokes. They liked to laugh … it's what was special about being a kid, as youngsters are known to laugh 400 times more every day than adults! The boys laughed at silly things and yucky things. And the yuckier and sillier those things were, the harder they laughed. Or just giggled … and sniggered until their sides were sore laughing.

Gorgeous George wasn't exactly gorgeous. He had one eyebrow higher than the other. One of his ears was slightly lower. It was just that some older girls kept calling him *Gorgeous* because his surname was also *Hansen*, or *Handsome Hansen*, as these mean girls teased.

His best friend, Kenny Roberts, could be described as slightly eccentric. Other people might just say that Crayon Kenny was stark raving bonkers. With a nickname like that, Kenny was famous, both in school and all around their home town of Little Pumpington for his unusual hobby of sticking crayons, Brussel sprouts, peas, cornflakes and pretty much anything else up his nose, and sometimes other places.

Most of the nurses and doctors at Little Pumpington General Hospital were on first name terms with his parents and it was rumoured that they had a special pair of forceps with Kenny's name on them. Crayon Kenny enjoyed the attention.

And, for the first time in these books, Grandpa Jock's dialogue (you know, the bits when he's speaking) will be written with his Scottish accent. This has been done, again by popular demand, to introduce more diversity to the text.

Here are a few examples, along with our easy-to-read translation for non-Scots readers:

Scottish Version	English Translation
How ye daein, laddie?	*How are you, young man?*
Aye, no' bad, how's yersel?	*Yes, I am rather well. How are you doing?*
Whaur dae ye come fae?	*Whereabouts do you live?*
Ah dinnae ken	*I do not know*
Whaur's yer lavvy?	*Where is your toilet located?*
Nae bother at a', pal	*That is no trouble at all, my friend*
Ta-ta ra noo	*Goodbye, for the moment*

And if you're struggling to read any of those words, just say them out loud in a really strong Scottish accent, and it will make complete sense.

Finally, one of the other main characters, Allison, has written her own chapters, from her diary, so nobody is left out. She can introduce herself later.

'What an absolute mess!' shrieked Allison, slamming her hands down onto her hips. 'It's a complete bomb site.'

Torn boxes were piled high. Newspapers were scattered around, blowing in the breeze of the children's footsteps. Empty cans of fizzy juice were stacked higgledy-piggledy in every corner. Large black bags were hanging from every rafter, and old clothes, hats and shoes were jumbled everywhere. Dust and fluff floated gracefully through the shafts of sunlight filtering into the loft.

'You might actually find a bomb up here,' giggled George.

'WHAT?' shrieked Allison again, not daring to move this time.

Crayon Kenny chuckled. 'You *have* met Mr Jock before, haven't you? You do know what that old geezer is capable of?'

Allison puffed up her cheeks and blew out a long breath. 'Yeah but I wasn't expecting him to keep live explosives up in his attic.'

'They'd probably be quite old,' sniggered Kenny. 'Wouldn't work anyway.' Allison was frozen to the spot. She looked around the attic, eyes searching, ears listening out for any tell-tale ticking.

'He's only kidding, Allison. Don't worry,' smiled George, his ginger hair catching in the cobwebs around the ceiling.

'Grandpa Jock threw out all his old grenades years ago. Anyway, that's not what we're up here for.'

'Well, what are we up here for?' sighed Allison, looking slightly less worried about where she should stand, and a bit more worried about the spider that was creeping into George's hair.

'Toilet paper, apparently.' Kenny sniffed, and his nostrils filled with the dust. He'd let it crust for a few minutes then pick it all out with his finger nail. George pointed over to a pile of boxes hidden behind the hanging suit carriers.

'What's in those boxes ... over there?' George pulled the carriers apart to reveal six large boxes, with little green crosses printed onto them. Each box read;

OSAL - Medicated Toilet Tissue.

'Jackpot!' shouted George, and he ripped open the top box. Inside, it was filled with dozens of smaller green boxes, each a little thicker than a video game case. They were covered thick with dust, and more little spiders scurried away into the darkness.

Allison stepped in closer with her torch. 'Mr Jock said we only needed one or two. Take a couple of boxes and let's get out of here ... this place is giving me the creeps.'

'Why does he want this old toilet paper, George?' Kenny shrugged, and scratched the inside of his nostril.

'No idea,' replied George, shaking his head and picking up two little boxes. 'He was talking about starting his own band.'

'With toilet paper?' asked Kenny, as he started towards the hatch-door, and the step-ladder below. George stepped forward with his prize, as Allison struggled behind hanging bags of clothes at the back.

'He did say there used to be a punk rock band called *Mark Skid and the Y-Fronts* but I've never heard of them,' said George, as he bumped into Kenny at the top of the stepladder.

'I'm sorry, George,' smiled Kenny.

'That's alright, mate. No need to …' George stopped walking and started coughing. He put his hand up to his face, covering his nose. The stench in his nostrils was almost burning. 'That's worse than rotten eggs. You're disgusting, man! Stop it!'

Kenny was giggling again. 'I'll stop doing it when you stop laughing!'

George began wafting his hands across the front of his face. 'That's… that's… that's *cabbage-esque!*'

'*Cabbage-esque?* You're just making words up now.'

George smiled and coughed again. '*Esque* means resembles or like or similar to. As in "your bottom smells like cabbage." *Cabbage-esque!* My grandpa says you can add *esque* to anything.'

'Right, what are you two laughing at?' announced Allison, smiling, as she fought her way through the coats, boxes and old newspapers. The boys were grimacing now, and Kenny winked across to George, who had put his hand over his mouth again.

Allison stepped passed George and Kenny, over to the stepladder and stopped. And turned. Her grin turned into a *Grrrrrr!* and the side of her lip curled upwards. She might've been about to sneeze, or even about to snarl, until the thick, warm air grabbed the back of her throat.

'Urrgh, not again,' she coughed.

Allison felt as if her nose and her mouth were coated with a gassy cloud of toxic gunk … this smell even tasted as if it had colour. Greens, and yellows and browns seemed to fill the heavy air, and her eyes began to sting. Allison felt as if she was breathing and eating the air at the same time. She desperately tried to wave the foul stench away, gasping for breath like a drowning swimmer. Until slowly the air began to clear and she could breathe freely once more.

'That's vile, boys,' she coughed again. 'I walked through that. You dropped one and I walked through it!'

'We call that *crop dusting*,' laughed George. 'It's like leaving a long trail of smelly smoke behind us... like bug spray from a plane... over a field. Just waiting for an unsuspecting victim.'

'I can't take credit,' sniggered Kenny. 'Simon and Edgar did it first.'

'You boys are all the same,' huffed Allison, as she stepped onto the first rung of the ladder. She looked up, and the boys had started shuffling and snapping their fingers.

'If the whole place honks,' Kenny started.

'And it don't smell good.' George joined in.

'Who ya gonna blame?'

'Crop Dusters!' shouted both boys together. George went on...

'And if the stench stinks bad,'

'In your neighbourhood'

'Who ya gonna blame?'

'CROP DUSTERS!' And the two boys began jigging and singing along to the little instrumental part of their song... 'Do-rood, do-rood, do-rood, do-rood, dood, dood, diddly'

'Do-rood, do-rood, do-rood, do-rood, dood, dood, diddly'...before the end of their song...

'I AIN'T 'FRAID OF NO POOP!' and boys fell into each other's arms, laughing.

Allison snatched the two green boxes of toilet paper out of George's hands and almost slid down the ladders from the loft into the fresh air below.

Chapter Two - Orange

Allison landed with a thump on the floor below, and took a step towards the stairs. She noticed, not for the first time, that Grandpa Jock's house was rather odd. She certainly knew that Grandpa Jock himself was rather odd but didn't realise how far that oddness extended.

The stair bannisters were painted orange; a deep, rich pumpkin and carrot colour.

The stair carpet was a weird orange zigzag pattern, with deep tiger stripes. Not an identical match to the paint but the colours clashed rather well together. Allison counted the steps as she went down. At the bottom she turned passed the front door and walked along the hall. The orange carpet continued.

As the hall opened into the living room, the carpet changed. The tiger orange pattern gave way to a solid block of dark rust-coloured carpet. The sofa was orange. There was a large, round, paper lamp shade hanging from the middle of the ceiling. Of course, it was orange too, like a giant tangerine. The cupboards, wall units and TV stand were made from smooth, rounded plastic - orange too, of course, and even the curtains were a shiny, marmalade colour. Luckily, the walls were covered in a white and green wallpaper with huge, jungle-like fern leaves. As Grandpa Jock might say, it was *rainforest-esque*.

And just then, Grandpa Jock walked through from the kitchen. His shock of fiery, orange hair around the sides of his head and his bushy moustache could've matched the curtains or the cupboards, or even the carpet.

And he didn't exactly walk. Grandpa Jock swaggered. He liked to swagger. His bright red kilt swayed from side to side with each step he took, and the old man seemed to take pride in this swish. He stopped in the middle of the room, and the corners of his mouth seemed to curl upwards, almost into a smile but it was hidden beneath his huge, ginger moustache.

'Ya beauty!' he shouted. 'You've found ma old toilet paper!'

Allison blinked with surprise and looked down at the small, green boxes in her hands. She offered them both to the old Scotsman.

'I didn't know that toilet paper came in boxes, Mr Jock.'

'Only the good stuff, lass,' said Grandpa Jock, his smile creeping out from beneath the hair on his top lip. 'And this stuff was the very best. Ah remember ma faither panic-buying tons of toilet paper … about a hundred years ago. Ah knew ah kept some.'

Allison paused, and was about to ask why anybody would want to panic-buy toilet paper, then she remembered what the shops were like at the start of the pandemic in 2020. People had gone a bit mad.

'Spanish flu, it was called back then.' Grandpa Jock was speaking but his hands were feverishly trying to rip open one of the boxes. With just enough pressure, the cardboard split and a flap appeared, revealing a pile of carefully folded tracing paper. Grandpa Jock folded the flap back and pulled out one sheet of paper with his fingers. It came out with a crunch.

'Osal medicated toilet tissue!' he announced. 'It was the best toilet paper money could buy, back in the day.'

'But that looks quite… er… crispy, Mr Jock,' said Allison, squinting. 'It doesn't look like soft tissue paper to me.'

Grandpa Jock chuckled. 'We were hardier back then. And huge sheets of this stuff were soaked with a germ-killing oil. Once it dried, it was cut up into smaller sheets, and packed into these little boxes. It was great for wiping yer bum!'

Allison did not look impressed. 'People wiped their bottoms … with tracing paper? Back in the old days?'

'Ah ha!' laughed the old geezer. 'No' just that. It was also great as a musical instrument.' And Grandpa Jock pulled out a comb from his sporran, and wrapped the sheet of stiff paper around it.

Editor's note

For goodness sake, Stuart, you need to tell your readers what a 'sporran' is! We've sold tens of thousands of books all over the world... Scotland, England, Ireland, Australia, Dubai, Hong Kong and India... you've even been a best-seller in the children's charts in Italy. But not everybody will know what a sporran is!

Okay, okay, I'll do it.

Little readers, a sporran is a leather bag that is worn around the waist, usually by Scotsmen. You see, kilts do not have pockets, so it is useful for keeping your phone and your car keys in. Or combs, in this case.

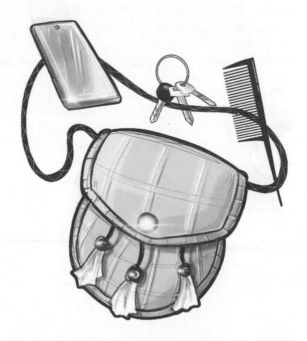

'Don't know why you need a comb, Grandpa. You don't have that much hair!'

George and Kenny had breezed into the living room and were watching Grandpa Jock fiddle with his comb and the crispy sheet of paper. It is true that the top of Grandpa Jock's head was completely devoid of hair, all shiny and polished like a snooker ball. However, what he lacked on the top he more than made up for around the back and sides of his head. Wild carrot-coloured hair poked out in all directions. Bushy sideburn whiskers, and a huge ginger moustache that often took on a life of its own.

'That's enough from you, boyo,' laughed Grandpa Jock. 'You'll be doing well if you have as much hair as I have when you're my age. Now, listen to this.'

And Grandpa Jock placed the toilet paper-wrapped comb underneath his moustache and began tooting. The paper, and the little teeth of the comb, started to vibrate with a high-pitched squealing. Then, as Grandpa Jock pushed his eyebrows together, the tone of the comb dropped to a deep, wavering *doo-doo-doo* before he picked up the pace.

Kenny and George started clapping along, and Grandpa Jock started kicking his little legs in tune with the music. At the end of his little legs were a pair of huge, clod-hopping boots, and his whole musical act was becoming dangerous. The old geezer was bouncing up and down, and bobbing his head furiously, still tooting and buzzing away on his comb. Occasionally, one of the boys would yell '*Yee-ha!*' and this seemed to push the old Scotsman on faster.

Allison just stared. She didn't know which tune Grandpa Jock was playing, or if indeed this really was actually music, but he was getting louder. And so were the boys.

'*Oh, When the saints … go marching in!*' Boom boom! They both sang and Allison's thoughtful little penny dropped.

George and Kenny had each picked up one of the green toilet paper boxes and were pretending they were tambourines, whacking them in time to the music and singing along. Grandpa Jock face was growing redder, as he built up to his big finale. He puffed his cheeks out, and finished with an impressive *Ta-daaaaa!* The boys were clapping furiously, and Allison thought they looked a couple of seals, slapping their flippers.

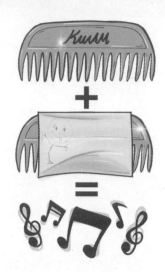

Grandpa Jock took a bow, and as he bent down, out slipped a toot of another sort.

'Oops,' he giggled. 'A little Johnny Squeaker,' and the boys giggled again. Grandpa Jock patted his stomach. 'Wholemeal bread, beans and prunes … just trying to stay regular.'

'Okay, okay, well done, Mr Jock,' Allison sighed, quickly changing the subject. 'You made a musical instrument out of toilet paper.' Was she mocking him?

'Cheaper than bagpipes, and better than a Playstation,' Grandpa Jock replied with a wink. 'Much easier to learn too. And ye dinnae need to use ma crunchy toilet paper. Ye could use tracing paper, or even grease proof paper, if ye wanted. Ma stuff just smells better, like moth balls. Here, you try.'

And the boys didn't need to be told twice, ripping into the boxes and whipping out fresh paper. Grandpa Jock pulled three combs from out of a drawer in the orange wall unit behind him, handed them to each child, (although Allison looked slightly disgusted), and the concert truly began.

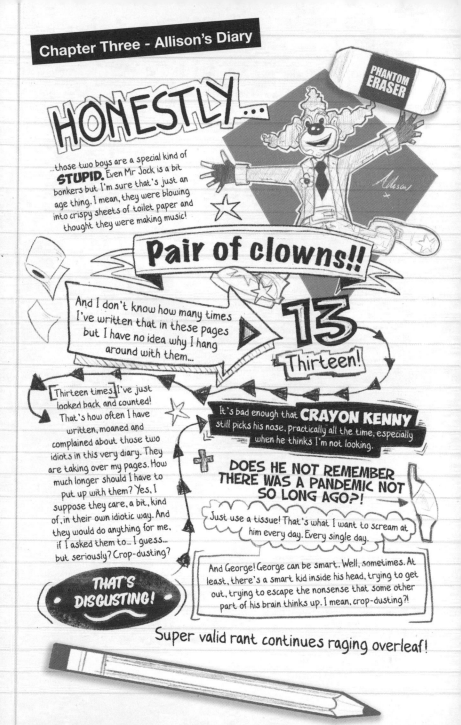

PHANTOM ERASER

HONESTLY...

...those two boys are a special kind of **STUPID**. Even Mr Jock is a bit bonkers but I'm sure that's just an age thing. I mean, they were blowing into crispy sheets of toilet paper and thought they were making music!

Pair of clowns!!

And I don't know how many times I've written that in these pages but I have no idea why I hang around with them...

13 Thirteen!

Thirteen times! I've just looked back and counted! That's how often I have written, moaned and complained about those two idiots in this very diary. They are taking over my pages. How much longer should I have to put up with them? Yes, I suppose they care, a bit, kind of, in their own idiotic way. And they would do anything for me, if I asked them to... I guess... but seriously? Crop-dusting?

THAT'S DISGUSTING!

It's bad enough that **CRAYON KENNY** still picks his nose, practically all the time, especially when he thinks I'm not looking.

DOES HE NOT REMEMBER THERE WAS A PANDEMIC NOT SO LONG AGO?!

Just use a tissue! That's what I want to scream at him every day. Every single day.

And George! George can be smart. Well, sometimes. At least, there's a smart kid inside his head, trying to get out, trying to escape the nonsense that some other part of his brain thinks up. I mean, crop-dusting?!

Super valid rant continues raging overleaf!

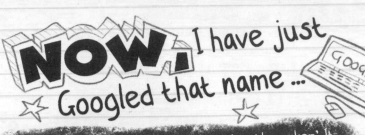

NOW, I have just Googled that name ...

GOOGLE

GEORGE. It means 'farmer' or 'earth worker'. It comes from the Greek. But if my George was a real farmer, then he would have to dust his crops to keep them healthy. But their version of crop-dusting is not healthy at all.

I remember they did it in school once ... leaving a stink like that in the corridor. Everybody was choking. Teachers were gagging, children were gagging, especially the smaller ones, whose noses were lower to the ground, and therefore closer to George's bottom, or Kenny's bottom, or whichever one of those two disgusting boys had dropped such a whopper!

And i had to stop writing to check this out, and i don't believe it.

I was hoping that 'Kenny' would mean 'bad smell' or something equally vile. I'm certainly not going to tell him this now. Kenneth means

'handsome'. SERIOUSLY

It is Irish for 'hand-some' or 'good looking' but he's the grottiest boy I have ever met. What does that say about Irish people?

Remember when mum and dad took me to Ireland for that holiday; it was great. We had so much fun, everybody was super-friendly, and I always said that I would love to go back. Well, I might need to reconsider that. I mean, if that nose-picking little monster is their idea of handsome, then Ireland may have other surprises.

BUT IT WAS FUN THOUGH! :)

I wonder what _my_ _na_me means?

Chapter Four - Crunchy

George and Kenny were lying sprawled out on the sofa, gasping for breath. Grandpa Jock slumped down into his favourite armchair and let his comb slip to the floor. His toilet paper was no longer crispy, now soaked with his drool and slobber.

Allison was still standing by the kitchen door, trying not to smile. She had, very carefully, blown a little *toot* into her comb and paper once or twice (it was kinda fun, and tickled her lips) but she couldn't stop thinking that the real purpose of the paper was to wipe people's bottoms.

'Mr Jock,' she asked. 'Who ever thought it was a good idea to make music with toilet paper?'

Grandpa Jock grinned. 'It was different back in those days, lass. We hud to make oor own entertainment. And we also hud a good laugh too.'

'Yeah, but I mean *toilet paper?*'

'That was the good stuff!' Grandpa Jock sat bolt up. 'George, did I ever tell ye about ma faither... I mean, your great-grandfaither? After the First World War... well, we called it The Great War back then because we didnae know there was going to be a second one, ma faither briefly hud a job as a toilet paper salesman, going door-to-door.'

'What? Going around people's houses with boxes full of bum wipes?' sniggered Kenny.

'Yeah, that's how it started,' smiled Grandpa Jock. He enjoyed surprising them with tall tales from long ago. 'Ye see, people were rather smelly back then in the olden days. They used to wipe their bottoms on strips of newspaper or old rags, or even handfuls of straw.'

Allison and George both made a **bleughhh** sound but Kenny just laughed.

'And then a chemist called Worrall Hall invented scratchy, soapy toilet paper. Smooth on one side, rough on the other, it was soaked with a germ-killing chemical, so it smelled fresh and zingy.' Grandpa Jock wiggled his fingers in front of his nose, as if smelling the paper for the first time.

'People said it was called *Osal* after Worrall's wife Sally. You see, when the inventor first tested his crunchy new paper, he shouted to his wife, "Oh Sal, I've ripped my bottom!" and the name *Osal* just stuck. And he soaked the sheets of paper in disinfectant for a bit longer, to make them a little bit softer.'

George screwed up his face. 'You mean they were crunchier than this?!' George scrunched another piece of toilet paper from the box. It sounded as if he were crushing a handful of dead leaves. 'It must've been like wiping your bum with a packet of crisps!'

'Aye, it was, laddie,' nodded Grandpa Jock. 'Ye had to scrape and scratch. It was like wiping yer butt with a glossy magazine, ye know, smearing rather than cleaning. Nowadays, you've all gone soft!'

'Soft? What do you mean soft, Grandpa?' George was pointing out towards the bathroom. 'You got packets of wet wipes in there!'

Kenny chuckled. 'Wet wipes? You know they're for babies, Mr Jock. My mum used them on my little brother!'

'Yes, Kenneth,' sighed Grandpa Jock. 'Bottoms get a bit more delicate as you get older. Sometimes ah'm just glad of the cooling, soothing glide of a baby wipe. That old stuff was course and brutal.'

'Do they still make the crunchy toilet paper, Grandpa?' George was still pulling out pieces of paper from the box and scrunching them in his hand.

'No, not any more, lad, but that was a problem in itself.' Grandpa Jock was now shaking his head. 'See, because people, mainly men, hud been used to rubbing their bottoms with this stuff.' He took a sheet from George and crunched it. 'And then new, softer toilet paper was introduced… like proper tissues, old guys still scraped hard but their fingers would always rip right through the softer paper. Grown men hud to be *trained* to wipe their bottoms gently without dirtying their hands.'

Allison turned to walk away, shaking her head. 'I really don't know how we got onto such a subject. It's hardly becoming of a lady.'

'You started it, Allison!' yelled the boys together.

'I certainly did not!' replied Allison, wrinkling up her nose.

'Yeah, ye did, lass,' nodded Grandpa Jock, sadly. 'Ye asked me about that new brand of chocolate spread I huv in the kitchen there, and…'

Kenny nudged George. 'Spreading the chocolate,' he giggled. 'That's what you get for using a glossy magazine!' And the lads high-fived each other.

Grandpa Jock ignored them. 'And ah said it was part of a big trial at the supermarket. They're filming a TV advert down at ma store, and we huv to test the stuff. And then ah said that the company who make it are called *Craftee*, big company, they make loads of things. One of their old products was **Osal - medicated toilet paper**. That's when ah remembered ma faither's old stock in the loft.'

'Oh yeah, that's right, Mr Jock. George told me you were working down at the supermarket,' said Allison, nodding. 'You are a Meeter & Greeter at the front door, aren't you? How are you enjoying your new job?'

'Ah hate it,' growled Grandpa Jock, his happy, sing-along mood disappearing in a flash. A dark look spread across his face. 'Well naw, ah just hate ma boss, Mr Spender. Ah wudnae wee on him if he was on fire!'

17

Chapter Five - Grim Reading

Grimley Spender was a horrible, little man.

All three of those things were correct. You might even say that he was an *absolutely* horrible, little man. Yes, he was a man, well, male anyway. Yes, he was short, and most definitely, he was horrible; a bitter, twisted, angry, little man in every way. You've heard of the phrase - *good things come in small packages?* Well, bad things come in even smaller packages too.

Grimley's friends would've called him *Grimm* for short but he didn't have any friends.

Well, he did have friends once but they'd all deserted him because of his rudeness, his petty and spiteful attitude and his habit of barking like a small dog when he spoke.

Not that he spoke that often. He usually just shouted. Grimley liked shouting at people. It made him feel bigger … and important. His name, *Grimley*, comes from the Old English word *grima*, which means 'goblin', and that suited him rather well.

This bad behaviour probably began when Grimley was a small boy (he's still a small man now but you know what I mean). He had two older brothers, who were both much taller than he was, so Grimley thought the only way to be noticed was to shout… and if that didn't work, shout louder … and then, EVEN LOUDER STILL!

He might still have two brothers but since he hadn't spoken to them for over twenty years Grimley couldn't be sure. Not that it bothered him.

And as a child Grimley didn't like school. He would shout at the other kids. The other kids would shout back at him. Then the teachers would shout, and Grimley would always end up in trouble, quite deserved too. The teachers tried very hard to help him but he didn't want to learn anything, so he left school when he was just fourteen. He actually left before the school could expel him (somebody had put dog poo on the handle of the staffroom door, and although they couldn't prove it, the teachers had their suspicions). In the end, Grimley leaving school was probably best for everyone.

So, no education, no manners, no dreams. But back in those days, supermarkets were quite a new thing, and were always looking for staff. Grimley applied for a job. Unbelievably, they gave him one. Pushing trolleys in the supermarket's car park.

The trouble was that Grimley couldn't reach much beyond the trolley's handlebars; he wasn't strong enough to push a line of trolleys uphill, and he certainly couldn't control a line of trolleys if they began to speed up downhill. It was after he had whacked his third parked car that he decided to do what he did best - SHOUTING!

He shouted at the other two trolley pushers, telling them that he'd been officially promoted to a new role called *Trolley Taskmaster and Basket Boss*. His voice was so loud and so commanding that the other boys just simply believed him, and he spent the whole day shouting at them to push harder and work harder, to make up for the trolleys that Grimley couldn't reach. Shouting was his gift.

Surprisingly, Grimley was married but no-one had seen his wife for years. She was said to be a lovely lady, or at least she had been, and that Grimley had tricked her into marrying him and now he keeps her locked up in his house. She certainly never comes out but people think she may need a wheelchair to get around nowadays, as two women in smart, blue tunics visited the house twice a day, every day. They were probably carers for Mrs Spender.

Some people had even heard shouting from inside the house. 'I'm not looking after her. That's your job!' It certainly sounded like Grimley Spender.

'Call yourself carers,' the rants would go on. 'You can't even make the bed!'

Over the years, Grimley had managed to fall out with all his neighbours. It was as if he enjoyed annoying people. He didn't like where people parked their cars. He didn't like the new windows that were fitted to one house. He didn't like the noise children made.

Once, Grimley bought some chickens, and built a chicken run for them at the bottom of his garden. You might think he liked fresh eggs, but Grimley told the postman that he hoped the chicken feed would attract rats! He wanted to irritate his neighbours with the rodents, and the chicken run was far enough away from his house to worry about them.

And because he was such a good shouter, he really was promoted by the supermarket. First, to supervisor, then to store manager. And as manager, Grimley bought himself a shiny, leather briefcase, and he liked to carry it around, to show how important he was.

In the olden days, supermarkets worked best with lots of shouting … and yelling, and screaming, and general bullying. Telling staff what to do was always necessary, and the louder you did it, the faster the job was done, or so it was believed.

Grimley Spender found his dream job! And it was a proud moment for the grouchy, little man. Store manager at the new All-Days Superstore in his home town of Little Pumpington!

Chapter Six - Grandpa Jock's Dairy

'So why do you still work there ... if your boss is such a horrible man?' asked Allison, as they all moved through to the kitchen. Grandpa Jock had opened up his biscuit barrel, and George and Allison helped themselves to the only biscuits in there, digestives. The crunchy toilet paper boxes were left discarded on the orange worktop.

'Don't you have any donuts, Mr Jock?' asked Kenny, politely.

'Just digestives, lad,' replied Grandpa Jock.

'Oh, okay,' grunted Kenny. 'I don't like digestives. They're probably old and soggy anyway.'

'Sounds like soor grapes to me, Kenny,' said Grandpa Jock firmly. 'All the more for us then.' He winked across to George and Allison. Allison's eyes glimmered.

'Soor?' humphed Kenny, folding his arms.

'Yeah, Kenny. It's Scottish for *sour*, like lemons. Just because we didn't have donuts.' George held the biscuit barrel out to Kenny, then pulled it away quickly before he could grab one. George laughed and offered the barrel out again, and Kenny snatched up a digestive and started munching. The biscuits were crisp, crumbly and delicious.

But Allison was not going to let her question go. She was worried. She liked Mr Jock, and wanted to help him with his bully of a boss.

'I mean, you're quite old, Mr Jock,' she went on, trying to be as nice as possible. Nobody really knew how old Grandpa Jock was but it was rumoured that he was between seventy-four and ninety-six. 'You don't really *need* to work.'

'Ah like working, lass. Ah mean, ah *usually* do.' Grandpa Jock's bushy moustache fluttered as he spoke. 'Ah like keeping busy. It's a good way to get out of the hoose. Ah love meeting people. Being paid to be a *meeter* AND a *greeter* was perfect for me. And ah've been working all ma life. Ah started when ah was thirteen.'

'That must've been *years* ago,' giggled George, wiggling his eyebrows. Grandpa Jock smiled as he flicked a little piece of digestive biscuit at his grandson for being cheeky.

'What was your first job, Mr Jock?' asked Allison, trying to keep the conversation sensible. She knew that if George and Kenny started their nonsense then the chit-chat would slide into chaos very quickly. Kenny had already started to pick his nose again.

'Ah used to deliver milk,' said Grandpa Jock, his eyes rolling upwards, as he thought back through the years. 'Ah had a cart and a donkey, and ah used to get up at four o'clock in the morning.' Kenny winced. The thought of wakening up at 4am was almost too painful for him.

'First thing every morning, ah'd load the cart with milk bottles down at the local dairy, harness up the donkey, Oaty ...'

'Oaty?' quizzed George. 'That's a strange name for a donkey.'

'Well, he liked eating oats ... and bran, and crunchy stuff like that,' Grandpa Jock nodded. 'To be honest, ah think he was a bit mad, as donkeys go. Very stubborn, always thought he knew best. He'd been at the dairy for years, so he knew the milk round better than any of the drivers.

Trouble was, Oaty wasn't too steady on his feet.'

Kenny nudged George, and whispered 'A wonky donkey.' Grandpa Jock pretended not to hear and went on…

'And he was really old. Like, he was even blind in one eye.'

'A winky wonky donkey?' giggled George, and Kenny sprayed biscuit crumbs out of his mouth as he laughed. George added, 'Did he have problems with gas, Grandpa? I mean, did Oaty the donkey pass wind at any time?'

Allison squinted at George through half shut eyes; she was onto him. Kenny was too, and George added, 'You mean, he was a stinky winky wonky donkey!' and Kenny burst out laughing. George chuckled at his joke and Allison just shook her head.

'Hay! Don't laugh at ma donkey, ya cheeky monkey,' shouted Grandpa Jock, but he was smiling so the boys knew they'd get away with it. 'Anyway, ah'm telling ye about ma milk round.'

'Just keep going, Mr Jock,' nodded Allison. 'Ignore those two clowns.'

'You're right, lass,' said Grandpa Jock, waggling his boney old finger at the boys. 'Ye see, it was quite dangerous, back in those days. Nobody worried about health and safety years ago, and ah was only thirteen, and in charge of the most stubborn donkey in the world. So ah had to show it who was boss.'

George had stopped sniggering. Kenny pulled his finger out of his nose, wiped it on his shorts, as both boys leaned forward. George had heard lots of his grandpa's stories and they were usually worth listening to.

'What did you do, Mr Jock?' asked Allison.

'Well, we were going oot one morning, and it was a very cold, ice everywhere.' Grandpa Jock's eyes were sparkling, and his fingers danced through the air, shimmering like ice crystals. 'There were no road gritters to put salt doon back then, and ma donkey slipped on an icy patch.'

'Aww … poor Oaty!' wailed Allison.

'Poor Oaty nothing,' grunted Grandpa Jock. 'He just crouched there, squatting, with his legs tucked underneath him, refusing to take another step. Ah mean, how was ah meant to deliver ma milk?'

'So what did you do, Grandpa?' said George, leaning further forward.

'Quick as a flash,' winked Grandpa Jock. 'Ah ran over to old Mrs McLuckie's hoose, just across the road. See, she kept chickens in her back garden, and ah knew she would be boiling eggs for her husband's breakfast. He was a shift worker and she was always boiling eggs early in the morning… cheap food back in the day. Her whole house stunk of boiled eggs.'

Grandpa Jock went on. '"Emergency, Mrs McLuckie, emergency!" ah yelled. "Ah need a boiled egg!" And without hesitation, the old dear came to the front window with a steaming hot egg on a spoon. Ah snatched the egg from her and ran back to ma donkey Oaty, juggling the egg from hand to hand so as not to burn masel'.'

'So you fed the boiled egg to the donkey?' asked George, screwing up his face.

'Naw, of course no'!' yelled Grandpa Jock. 'Ah lifted its tail and shoved the egg up Oaty's bottom!' The three children's jaws dropped open, faces aghast.

'And the donkey was off like a rocket, charging down the street as if he was being chased by the Devil himsel',' grinned Grandpa Jock, looking very pleased with himself. 'Fastest milk round in the history of the dairy!'

George and Allison turned to stare at each other in awe, their jaws still hanging open. Kenny, on the other hand, although still looking rather shocked, had been thinking. A puzzled expression was slowly spreading across his face, and that was never a good thing. Allison glanced over at

25

him, and began to worry. Kenny was the most disgusting boy she had ever met, and there was a good chance that whatever he was thinking about, it was probably yucky.

'Mr Jock?' queried Kenny. *Oh no, here it comes.* 'Whatever happened to the egg?'

Allison breathed a sigh of relieve. That could've been worse.

'Oh, at the end of ma milk round ah just ate it for ma breakfast,' replied Grandpa Jock, with a smug grin. *It was worse!* George gagged and pretended to be sick. Allison puffed her cheeks out and made a bobbing noise in her throat. Kenny's eyes almost popped out of his head.

Seeing their faces, Grandpa Jock tried to explain. 'Well, it was still warm! And ah didn't eat the shell, obviously. The actual egg bit was *inside* the shell!'

George gagged again. 'No, Grandpa, it was *inside* a donkey's bottom.'

'At least you showed the donkey who was boss, Mr Jock,' said Kenny, trying to regain his composure.

'Eggs-actly!' replied Grandpa Jock, wiggling his incredibly bushy eyebrows again.

!!! Editor's note - Warning !!!
Do not stick boiled eggs up donkeys' bottoms. Or horses' bottoms, or dogs' bottoms, or cats', or even your little brother's bottom, no matter how annoying he might be.

PHANTOM ERASER

DIARY UPDATE...

Yes, I'm having that. I am DEFINITELY taking that one.

← #WANT

Allison means 'noble'. Like a queen or a duchess.

Yes, I like that. I am definitely noble. The website also said that 'Allison was also commonly associated with the adorable French nickname Aalis.' Yes, noble and adorable! I am totally suited to my name.

ARE THESE HEAVY?

Allison (Wonderland, George calls me) - a well-travelled name, it says, Allison must be honest and humble. Not sure about being well-travelled (but I've been to loads of different schools) however, I am certainly honest. And if I think I am noble and adorable, can I be humble too? Okay, why not? It is my name after all.

Although, it might be hard to be humble tomorrow. It's the big football final at our school's sports day. My house team is playing last year's champions but of course, I wasn't playing last year. I just might make the difference.

Wait ... Hang on. Humble, Allison, **THINK HUMBLE**

Actually, no. If I'm being honest, I am definitely better than most of those boys

TRUTH BOMB

Think honestly!

Chapter Eight - Sports Day

As usual, Little Pumpington Primary School had organised its sports day on the coldest, wettest, most miserable day of the summer so far. The summer holidays were still a few days away, and the sun had been shining for the last three weeks but now that sports day had arrived, the skies opened.

As depressing as it was to sit inside a classroom and watch the glorious sunshine warm the world outside, it was even worse to be standing in a cold, wet playing field, dripping with rain water, watching dozens of drenched children play games round about you. The teachers at Little Pumpington Primary School insisted that children go outside to play sports, regardless of the weather. *Character building*, they called it.

George stood on the football pitch, in his all-blue strip, roughly in the position he thought he should stand as the team's left-back.

'Left back in the dressing room, more like,' Kenny would always shout, thinking he was clever but, as goalkeeper, he was no better, dwarfed beneath a set of towering full-sized goalposts at the end of the pitch.

George looked around at the different games going on with the other classes. There was the usual egg and spoon race for the younger children. *I'll bet none of those eggs have been near a donkey's bottom*, he smiled. There was a balloon and spoon race for the even smaller children, who had all given up trying to balance the balloon on their spoon, and were using their hands to hold it in place.

Lastly, there was a new game for the in-between kids. Trickier than the egg and spoon race but not as easy as the balloon and spoon, the children here had carefully balanced what looked like a small, black pebble on a tablespoon. It was shiny and wrinkled, and George puzzled for a second. *Of course,* he thought *the prune and spoon race!* He

had to admire the teachers' imaginations, and finding a
special way to trick children into eating healthily, as most
of the kids had given up balancing their prunes and were
munching heartily on them.

'Man on, George,' screamed Allison from further up the
pitch. 'Close him down!'

George, who had never really been interested in football,
had absolutely no idea what those words meant. Allison
might've been speaking a foreign language for all he knew.
But he looked up, just in time to see a huge, lumbering
giant of a player, in an all-white kit, charging towards him
with the ball.

Since he couldn't decide whether to dodge left or duck
right, George stood exactly where he was, as the big lad
smashed over the top of him, knocking him to the ground.
George landed face first in the biggest puddle on the pitch.
Of course, it wasn't really a watery puddle, more of a thick
gloopy swamp, and George heard a little voice at the back
of his mind saying *Hope there's no poo in this puddle*. The
people of Little Pumpington were not the most thoughtful,
and preferred to allow their dogs to poo on any patch of
grass they could find.

George lifted his head, mud dripping from his face. The
giant was a boy called Jude Spender, who always wore
no.9 on the back of his shirt, as he ran around Kenny
with the ball and slotted it into the back of the net. *Not
another goal*, groaned George. Jude kept running, arms
outstretched, milking the cheers from the small crowd.

'Come on, boys!' yelled Allison. 'I can't do it all myself.
I've scored three goals already and we're still getting beat.'

George dropped his head back into the puddle and
blew bubbles of dirty mud out of his mouth. Allison was
right. She was the best player in their team; faster and
more skillful than any other kid on the pitch, but this still
wasn't enough.

Their goalscorer, the big no.9, Jude Spender, was over-doing his lap of honour as usual, waving his hands in the air and asking the crowd to cheer louder. The fans, on the other hand, were clapping with more enthusiasm than they wanted, mainly because Jude was a big guy, and whatever Jude wanted Jude usually got. Or there would be trouble!

As he ran back to the centre circle, Jude deliberately trod on the back of George's head, pressing his face further into the mud. Jude sneered, 'Know who you look like? Messi. Haha, you get it? Messy.' And he laughed at his own joke all the way into the other half of the pitch.

'Please blow the whistle, ref,' George muttered. And as if taking pity on the losing team the referee blew for full-time. The game had finished four-three, and the players were now gathering in the middle of the pitch.

'Not as bad as last year,' panted Kenny, as he trotted to join his team mates. Allison shook her head. In the centre circle, the school janitor was busy wheeling out a small podium. The stand had a banner across the front, which read *All-Days Supermarket - Sponsors of Little Pumpington Primary School Sports Day*.

'Not as bad? It was close but we could've done better!' hissed Allison. 'We should've stopped at least two of their goals. And they shouldn't just give us medals for turning up.'

A parade of players, all wearing white kits, were forming a line at the front of the podium, and their new headteacher walked up with a large silver trophy. Of course, Jude Spender, as self-appointed team captain, was at the front of the queue.

'I can't watch this,' groaned George, and he turned to walk inside. As he did so, he passed another table sponsored by the All-Days Supermarket. This time the table was piled high with little jars of brown paste, each with a red and yellow label across the front with brown lettering.

The sign above read *New Product* and *Try Me - You'll love it*.

The banner across the front of the table was printed with the words **Spr3d The Chocolate.**

This sign annoyed George. First, *Spr3d* wasn't spelled properly. It used the number three instead of the two middle vowels. Spread should always be spelled *spread*, thought George. And the number three was smeared to look like a knife spreading chocolate paste across a slice of bread.

Some companies just try to be too smart, thought George again. But the sign did say *Try Me* so George whipped a little jar away from the table discreetly, as he sauntered passed, trying to look casual.

Chapter Nine - Jude's Law

Jude Spender was a bully. And not just the type of bully who would pull girls' hair (although he would do that too). Jude would kick small boys up the bottom so hard that the small boys would actually take off, both feet completely off the ground.

With older children, he would walk behind them and clip one of their feet, so the poor kid would trip themselves. And then, he would laugh at them; a sneering, nasty giggle that came out of his nose.

Jude would also spit in people's hair, again as he walked behind them. He was sneaky like that. And not just normal spit but the horrible green, lumpy stuff. Here, he wouldn't laugh. He would just turn away, so as not to get caught. He would ping children's ear lobes. He would lick his finger and stick the wet tip right into little kids' ears. It was disgusting. Jude was disgusting!

And he was bigger than all the other kids in Little Pumpington Primary School. He was even taller than his dad. And he was only twelve. Some people thought that was odd because Grimley Spender was quite a small man but Jude had just kept growing and growing and growing.

However, Jude did have one big advantage over the other children; he was in fact two years older than everyone else in his class (except the teacher, obviously). His dad had kept him out of school for a couple of years because Grimley Spender thought he knew more than the teachers, so decided to home-school his son. But Grimley wasn't a teacher, and he soon grew bored of teaching important stuff like reading, and writing, and counting, so he gave up, and Jude was left to look after himself.

Once Little Pumpington Council realised that one of their children was missing from class Jude was whisked away to be checked and tested, and tested and checked, then tested some more. Finally, it was decided that Jude needed to finish primary school properly before going on to secondary school. So he was put into George's class just two weeks before the summer holidays.

And that's how this towering bully came to think he could rule the school!

JUDE SPENDER

Chapter Ten - Spreading The Chocolate

'Championeee! Championeee! was me, was me, was me!'

Sports day was finished... well, it was just sports morning really, and all the pupils had moved back inside to their classrooms before lunch. Jude, however, was still celebrating his team's success by dancing up and down between the rows of desks. Well, actually, as usual Jude was just celebrating his own personal success, and completely ignoring the efforts of his team-mates but nobody wanted to mention that to the biggest kid in the school.

Little Pumpington Primary School did have changing rooms next to the playing fields but some council bosses thought sports were just an excuse for children to skip lessons. The time it took to wash, dry off and put on clean clothes only meant less time away from their classroom, and less time away from their *real* education. Although considered a distraction, legally, sports had to be part of the timetable. Drying off and cleaning up was not.

So, as the children were walking back to their desks, they were dripping, soggy and very, very wet. Steam could be seen rising from the top of their heads. Puddles were forming beneath their feet, as they sat at their desks. Chairs were being dragged through those puddles, and water was splashing everywhere.

Most of the children had already sat down when George walked up to Jude, who was still standing, grinning and waving to what he thought were his adoring fans.

'Thank you. Thank you,' he went on, nodding his fake approval. He grabbed the back of his chair and pulled it out.

'That will do, Jude. Sit down please,' said Miss Mack sternly. Miss Mack had been George's teacher for the whole year, but of course, she had only been Jude's teacher for less than two weeks. It had been hard work helping Jude readjust to school life again.

But right before he could sit down, George stepped up to the big kid and offered him his hand. 'Well played, Jude. Good game,' George nodded.

Jude smiled. 'I'd say the same back but you lot were rubbish,' he sneered, leaving George's hand hovering in the air. George held eye contact, although Jude's eyes were much higher. Reluctantly, Jude fist-bumped George's open hand and sat down.

'Yeah, whatever,' groaned Jude rudely, and George returned to his seat with a smile.

'What was all that about?' whispered Kenny, as they sat together. He pointed down towards Jude, who was sitting awkwardly on a chair that was clearly two sizes too small for him. There was now steam rising up from the shoulders of his white football top, as his body heat began to dry off his shirt. His white shorts were dripping into little puddles on the floor and his dirty white socks were rolled down around his ankles.

'Shhhh,' whispered George. 'You'll see later.' And he winked at Kenny with a huge grin. Lunch time could not come soon enough for both boys.

Eventually, the bell rang and every pupil stood up, slid their chairs beneath their desks and shuffled towards the door. Except Jude, who was pushing and shoving the smaller kids out of his way. He always had to be first to the dinner hall.

But George hadn't moved. He gently pulled Kenny's elbow back, and pointed towards the door. 'Wait for it,' he whispered. 'Wait for it.'

And then, as Jude marched towards the door, Kenny finally saw what George wanted him to see.

There was a large, brown stain down the back of Jude's white shorts. It was dark and thick, and smeared right between the cheeks of his bottom.

'Has he … has he poo'd himself?' stammered Kenny, holding onto George's arm. George was chuckling quietly, his shoulders bouncing up and down with silent mirth. Kenny giggled too. Then they both laughed. They looked again at Jude's dirty shorts, just as he reached the door, and the boys howled uncontrollably, great guffaws bursting out of their mouths.

'Look,' cried Allison, who was closer to the front of the class. 'Jude's had an accident in his pants.'

The bully stopped and turned back. The classroom was a sea of smiling, laughing faces, not laughing with him this time but laughing at him. Jude twisted his back to try to see behind him, to see what everybody else thought was so funny, and he whirled around in a circle. His arm reached round his back, and he felt the thick, sticky splodge on his bottom. His fingers sunk right into the mess, and he pulled his hand back. There was brown gunk beneath his finger nails.

He didn't remember losing control of himself. He certainly did *not* remember taking a dump in his underpants, in the classroom! He hadn't done that since he was five. Instinctively,

Editor's note
Stuart, that's a big word for little readers.
Let me help. Try to spell it out, kids.
In - stink - tiv-ly   in - stink -tiv-ly
Oh I see, Stuart, very funny! You just wanted
*to use a big word with **STINK** in the middle. Okay,*
okay, carry on, little readers. Nothing to see here.

Instinctively, Jude put his fingers up to his nose and
sniffed. The children in front of him all laughed and barfed,
and bleughed their tongues out, pretending to be sick
at the sight of the oldest kid in the class sniffing the poo
from his pants.

'It's just chocolate,' he shouted, trying to explain the
situation. He really was innocent but all the kids saw were
brown stains from his butt on his fingers and poo smears
on his shorts. Everybody was laughing at him, including the
teacher, who was trying to cover her face with her hands.

'It's just chocolate spread!' Jude shouted and he sniffed
his hand again. 'LOOK!' he yelled, and he started licking his
fingers to prove his point. The whole classroom lost control.

Whoops, laughs, groans and barfs sprayed out from
the crowd. Children held their tummies, as their sides
were being split. The laughter was becoming rowdy and
boisterous, even girls-terous, as children fell about in
helpless fits of giggles.

Editor's note
Right, Stuart, that's enough. GIRL-STEROUS?! Really?
You are just making words up now.

Boisterous? Girl-sterous? Even teacher-sterous? It didn't
really matter because the valve had cracked. The tense,
nervous mood that always surrounded Jude Spender had

broken apart. No-one had ever wanted to upset Jude before but now it felt as if there was safety in numbers. Everybody was laughing, and let's be honest, it looked as if Jude had just eaten his own poo!

It was at that point, Jude exploded!

Chapter Eleven - Almost Stung!

'We should be okay here for a while,' said George softly, as he wiped up the trickle of blood dripping down from Allison's ear. The three children had retreated into the woods behind the school, and were hiding behind a large fallen tree; its base up-ended and now a mass of twisted roots, earth and mud. It had stopped raining but the ground was still soggy.

'And he'll soon forget,' nodded Kenny. 'We can sneak back to the school then.'

'How will he forget?' snapped Allison. 'The whole school is laughing at him, and he's walking around with a huge poo-cake on his shorts.'

'We were right to make a run for it though,' added George. 'I think we touched a raw nerve there.'

'Raw nerve? He went bananas! I've never even seen that gorilla before last week,' Allison went on. 'And just because he spreads chocolate on his fingers and we all laugh at him, that vicious monkey tries to pull my earrings out.'

'Yeah, sorry Allison,' George said sadly. 'That was kinda my fault. It was me who covered his chair with chocolate spread.'

'Ahhhhh, and then you distracted him with your handshake,' realised Kenny, nodding approval. 'So he wouldn't see the mess you'd spread when he sat down. Genius, George. Absolute genius.'

The three youngsters stood quietly for a few minutes, trying to pull their thoughts together; they were still shaking. They knew they shouldn't be in the woods, or even beyond the front gate or the fence during school hours but that incident in class had been scary. In time, Allison stepped over the tree trunk and was about to sit down.

'Watch where you're sitting, Allison.' Kenny pointed to the mass of green stems and thick leaves sprouting out from

YEAH, SORRY ALLISON. THAT WAS KINDA MY FAULT. IT WAS ME WHO COVERED HIS CHAIR WITH CHOCOLATE SPREAD...

the bottom of the tree stump.

'Urgh ... Jaggy nettles,' yelled George. And Allison jumped back.

'Jaggy nettles?' giggled Kenny. 'They're called stinging nettles, George.'

'My Grandpa Jock calls them *jaggy* nettles,' replied George rather abruptly. 'Because they jag you. You know, that's just the same as stinging.'

Allison stepped back across to where the lads were standing. She looked around the clearing, and saw that there were nettles growing everywhere. Kenny stepped across and pressed a large clump of them down with his foot. The stems snapped and bent backwards, as Kenny kicked them underneath the tree trunk. He then took his jacket off and threw it across the trunk, making sure there were no nettles sticking out.

'I hate them,' she spat. 'I think they're evil. They burn,

and sting, and Urghh! Look, they're everywhere!'

Nobody had noticed how many nettles were growing around the tree trunk when they first arrived but now they took their time. There were bushes of nettles everywhere, growing in the damp shade of the trees.

'My grandpa says they're good for you, if you're not stung,' nodded George. 'He says you can eat them in salads, or cook them, or even make tea from them. In the past, they were used as medicine.'

'Urgh, can you imagine?' choked Kenny. 'Putting a stinging nettle into your mouth. Your lips and tongue would blister and burn. It would be like the spiciest curry ever!'

'I think you soak the nettles in water first, before you eat them. That removes the stinger parts. Or you should just grab them firmly, and that crushes the sharp hairs that sting you.'

'Well, I'm still not touching them,' humphed Allison, folding her arms to keep her fingers away from the clawing, green stems. 'You just need to brush against the leaves, and it's like a burst of fire. Hot, and sharp and so blooming painful.'

George smiled sadly. 'It's like being too close to Jude,' he said. 'It was my fault but you got stung!' The children stopped talking, and stood in silence for a few seconds, thinking.

When Jude exploded he launched himself at Allison in a rage. She wasn't the closest person to him but she was the last to speak to him. In Jude's mind, Allison caused his embarrassment, and he wanted her to pay for it. He had grabbed her by the ears and tried to rip out her gold studs. Luckily, Miss Mack had pulled Jude off quickly, and marched him out of the classroom towards the Headteacher's office. It all happened so fast, and that was when all the children scarpered.

Of course, Jude didn't actually *explode*.

There were no little bits of Jude that needed to be scraped off the ceiling. There was no puddle of Jude on the floor, and nobody had to pick sticky bits of Jude out of their hair. It was not that kind of explosion.

But Jude did go *ballistic* though. He hated being laughed at, and standing in front of the whole class with poo-like chocolate on his shorts had tipped him over the edge. He could've laughed it off, if he had a sense of humour but Jude only enjoyed laughing at other people's misfortune. He was the first to laugh if someone tripped over. He was often to blame for the tripping. He would pick on people for their height, or their weight, or their clothes, or the way they spoke, or the size of their nose, or ears or feet. Anything to be mean.

Allison said she thought this was a distraction, to stop people looking too closely at Jude himself. His behaviour was usually that of a four-year-old, and he had to get his own way all the time. He had to show off his strength. He liked to frighten and intimidate smaller kids, to show how big he was. Allison thought that perhaps Jude was actually insecure, perhaps even scared of life and the world around him.

So when Jude went ballistic, he was showing that he needed to be in control, and using anger to take it back, like a four-year-old.

Chapter Twelve - Who Wipes The Bums

Editor's note

*Well of course there is a **YUCK ALERT** for this chapter! Even the title has the word* Bums *in it, and not just one bum but multiple bums - sorry.*

'My little brother Johnny was like that, before he started school,' said Kenny, feeling important that he could actually add to the conversation. 'He calmed down a bit when he learned how to behave around other kids his own age.'

'That's mainly Jude's problem,' Allison added. 'I think he's been spoiled.'

'Well, we kinda knew that about Jude too … from before,' shrugged George. 'He was in another class a couple of years ahead of us and he always picked on the younger kids. Then he disappeared. Now we've caught up with him.'

'We haven't caught up with him, George,' sniggered Kenny, shaking his head. 'We might be in the same class with him now but he's still stretching ahead of us. He's huge!'

Allison squeezed the tissue around her ear lobe and held it there. The blood had stopped but she didn't want it to start again. She nodded her head in thanks to George for his tissue… since she certainly wasn't going to get a tissue from Kenny. He thought that's what sleeves are for.

'But where has he come from? He only arrived at school last month,' said Allison. 'And how does everybody know about him?'

'He had a reputation before. A real nutter,' replied George. 'Remember when he filled his teacher's desk drawer with paint?'

Kenny's eyes widened, and he slapped his forehead with the palm of his hand. 'Oh yeah, what a disaster. Everybody was slipping and sliding once the stuff all leaked out. The teacher even landed on her bottom.'

'And what about the time when he climbed out the classroom window and ran away!'

Kenny giggled. 'And not just that, Allison. His classroom was on the second floor!'

Allison gasped, and Kenny nodded his head. 'The boy's antics were legendary in the playground. As George says, a proper nut-case.'

George giggled this time. 'Do you remember when his class went on their school trip. To the big swimming pool? You know the main one with high diving boards?'

'Yeah, yeah, yeah,' Kenny was rocking back and forth now. 'And he climbed the biggest board, the big 10-metre one. And he jumped off.'

Allison's jaw was almost hitting the floor now. George's eyes were popping out of his head, and he added. 'Best bit was he did a proper belly flopper! Landed flat on his tummy. His stomach, and his chest and the front of his thighs were bright red for a week!'

Allison shook her head, and smiled. 'He's not the smartest cookie in the box, this Jude guy?'

'I think the teachers blame his parents,' said Kenny. 'They never really brought him up very well. They reckon his mum molly-coddles him too much and his dad just ignores him. My mum says that Jude is just looking for a reaction. You know, attention seeking.'

'Just after he started school, so he'd be about five years old, I heard that he couldn't use a knife and fork in the dinner hall,' George added. 'Ate his lunch with his fingers.'

'And I heard that lunch one day was mince, then custard! Imagine eating mince and custard with just your fingers.' Kenny winced, but Allison guessed that he'd maybe tried it.

George went on. 'So, he didn't know how to hold a pencil.'

'Couldn't tie his own shoelaces,' added Kenny.

'They say he wasn't even toilet trained,' giggled George. 'Aged five! He still wore those pull-up nappies.'

'No, no, no,' spluttered Kenny excitedly. 'Tell Allison about the *real* toilet story.'

Allison flicked her head around to look at George, who was standing laughing, his hand covering his mouth. Then he bent forward, beckoning them into a huddle.

'My big sister told me this one,' he whispered with a smile. 'She was older than Jude but the whole school was talking about it at the time.' Kenny giggled and nodded his head, (he'd heard this before) as Allison's eyes darted between the boys. George steadied himself, and coughed to clear his throat.

'Ahem. As I said, his parents didn't really teach him much when he was younger,' George smiled. 'Things like tying laces and holding pencils were the school's job, his dad said.'

George continued. 'So, not long after Jude started school, the teachers had to toilet train him to do a wee properly, and they had gotten rid of his pull-up pants.'

'So he didn't have to sit in the class with a nappy full of wee,' laughed Kenny.

'… And one day, Jude put his hand up and asked his teacher if he could go to the toilet. The teacher thought *that's a good step forward* so she let him go off by himself. Five minutes went by. Ten minutes went by. Then fifteen and the teacher began to worry. *What had happened to young Jude?* she thought.' George was milking his story now.

'And just as the teacher was about to go look for Jude, the classroom door bursts open. Bang!' George slammed his hands apart widely. 'And little Jude was standing there, with his shorts and his new pants around his ankles, and he shouts at the top of his voice...

Author's note

I thought that last chapter was quite good, and it certainly made me laugh, but in the next part the editor seems to have gotten carried away with his social responsibilities. You do not need to read the following page; it has nothing to do with the story.

However, Ed does make a few good points.

Editor's note

- Apologies to teachers here for such graphic imagery and the dangers of late-development toilet training. However, this is very likely a true story, told to Stuart in a staffroom by a teacher. This teacher was NOT the teacher in the story but 'a friend of a friend.'

And congratulations to all the excellent parents out there for correctly toilet training their children before the age of three... at the latest! Well done, take a sticker! 😃
(Stickers can be requested from @StuartReidBooks)

However, a message to those few parents whose children are still running around in pull-up nappies at the age of FIVE years old. Don't be lazy! Take some responsibility! Of course, due to certain medical conditions, some children don't have a choice about pull-up pants, and that's okay. Respect to those kids for facing up to all the challenges that life throws at them. And their parents too, for their patience, resilience and determination. I just want to call out those lazy parents who can't be bothered to teach their children important life skills.

It's not the school's job to teach your children self control! It's not the school's job to teach your children how to tie their own shoes laces. Or correctly hold their pencils, knives and forks.

AND GET OFF YOUR PHONES!

Get off your phones and talk to your children. They just want your time and attention!

Editor's note Part 2

Again, apologies for going off on one there but Stuart has just informed me about a chat he had with a Speech and Language Therapist who told him that the number of pupils who start school unable to speak properly, even pronounce their own names, has trebled in the last few years. And it's because some parents are not engaging with their children.

Kids, chances are that if you are reading this, then that's not you! Your mum and/or dad (and/or significant adult) have taken the time to instil in you a love for reading, and for books and stories - BRILLIANT! Children who receive regular bedtime stories, and become active readers, earn thousands of pounds more per year than non-readers by the time they turn thirty.* You kids can thank your mum and dad** when you're older!

Mums and dads** should be singing songs, telling nursery rhymes, making up silly voices, just talking and engaging with their children, even when they are tiny little babies. Little babies and toddlers love that stuff. They just want your time and attention. Give them the best start in life possible.

And mums and dads,** put your phones away at the school gates. Let your children tell you how exciting their day has been. You are the highlight of their little life. Your Facebook, Twitter, TikTok, Whats-App, Instagram, or whatever their silly names are, can all wait!

You will never get that special time back with your children when they are young. And I promise, you will miss it when it's gone.

Here endeth the lesson.

*Books are Forever: Early Life Conditions, Education and Lifetime Earnings in Europe by Giorgio Brunello, Guglielmo Weber and Christoph T. Weiss.

Published in The Economic Journal by the Royal Economic Society.

**and/or significant adult.

Illustrator's note

Wow, Ed. You really went off on one there. Here's a silly picture to lighten the mood. (of me!)

Chapter Thirteen

- The Angriest Little Man In The World

The afternoon in school ended much quieter than the morning had. George, Kenny and Allison crept back into the playground without being spotted by teachers or pupils, or at least, one pupil in particular. And Jude didn't come into class at all that afternoon.

By the end of the day, the three amigos felt almost free, apart from the lingering doubt that *revenge* might pop its head up at some point. To take their minds off it, they decided to walk to All-Days, their local superstore, to treat themselves to a cheeky bar of chocolate (Kenny said he wanted two donuts, maybe three, if they were on offer) and they'd maybe bump into Grandpa Jock, if he was working today.

All-Days was a giant of a supermarket chain, probably called 'All-Days' because they opened *all day*, and most of the night too. They had hundreds of stores all around the country, and the biggest shop in Little Pumpington had opened a few months ago. It sat at the north end of the town, not too far from the Little Pumpington Primary. This was handy for most families with children at the school but put Kenny dangerously close to a new source of donuts. He loved them.

In fact, Crayon Kenny's strange habit of putting crayons, peas, marbles and pretty much anything else up his nose started with donuts!

Erm ... well, not actually putting *donuts* up his nose. That would be silly. He'd been feeding a bag of donuts to elephants at the zoo, watching the animals pick the donuts up with their trunks. He'd gone home and tried sniffing sweets up his nostrils from the floor. And Kenny's odd little habit began there. (See *Gorgeous George and his Stupid Stinky Stories*).

As they approached, the store looked amazing. It was bright and colourful, with lights and flashing signs, and adverts selling all types of exciting foods. The trolley bay was sparkling too, as if some poor kid had been in there all night polishing every trolley with a toothbrush. Even the bins were gleaming.

Walking up to the entrance, the automatic doors shushed open with a relaxing whoosh. The next set of sliding doors slipped open effortlessly, not even a sound. Everything felt so in control, so modern, so hi-tech. Grandpa Jock was standing in the foyer, wearing his green All-Days t-shirt that matched his kilt.

'Welcome tae All-Days,' he smiled, meeting and greeting everybody who entered the shop. 'Special offer in aisle two today, madam, just for you.'

'Welcome tae All-Days,' Grandpa Jock went on. 'There's a big TV with yer name on it, sir. Over there in the Electronics section.' He looked like he was having fun, and then he spotted the kids.

'HEY HEY!' he yelled, dancing on the spot. 'My favourite shoppers! There's a donut deal in the bakery section, Kenny. Fill yer boots.'

'Bye, Jock. See you tomorrow.' A young man, no more than 18-years old, walked past with his head down, and his shoulders slumped. His feet shuffled, as if he was too tired to pick them up properly.

'Oh aye, ta-ta ra noo, Glen,' replied Grandpa Jock, waving after the young man.

Editor's note

See, you should've read the ~~Prologue~~, I mean the Introduction!

52

'That's Glen Pearce,' said Grandpa Jock pointing, as if he needed to explain. 'Poor lad, he's exhausted. Been working the night shift, polishing trolleys. Not the sharpest tool in the box but he's a hard worker, a good guy.'

George looked doubtful, *polishing trolleys?* Kenny and Allison exchanged glances. But more and more people kept pouring into the shop, and Grandpa Jock was in full flow, repeating his meeting and greeting to everyone. The children stepped back behind a large product unit to allow the old Scotsman to do his thing.

'Welcome tae the store, young lady,' he said again for about the 300th time that day. George didn't think the lady was that young but she smiled and nodded. The boy alongside her just stuck his tongue out.

'And ah know whit you would like, wee man,' Grandpa Jock grinned, and the child looked excited. 'You'd like to spread the chocolate, wouldn't ye?' he said, standing back to reveal a huge display of **Spr3d the Chocolate** chocolate spread jars. Large signs read *Special Offer, New Product and Try Me - You'll Love it!* The red and yellow jars were piled so high on the unit that no customer could ignore it when they walked into the store. Until a flame of ginger popped out from the behind the stand...

'Mum!' shouted Kenny, as he stepped out from behind the display. 'Mum, we're over here!' And he ran over to chat. George and Allison followed.

'Hiya Kenny,' squeaked the little boy waving madly, who, with his fiery red hair, looked remarkably similar to the older boy. The youngster was wearing a Batman t-shirt, blue shorts and a dirty pair of trainers. His nose was running with two green streaks of snot dripping down.

'That's my mum, Mr Jock. And my little brother, Johnny.' Grandpa Jock nodded his greeting to them, as George and Allison stepped closer to fist bump the little fellow, who clearly knew them well.

'Mum, Mum, Mum,' whined Johnny. 'Can I go with Kenny? And Allison and George. I'll be good. I'll be really good. I promise. Pleeeeeeeaaaaaaaazzzzzzzz!?'

Johnny had only been out of school for an hour, and his mum was looking a little frazzled around the edges. Kenny was bonkers but at least he was calm about it. His younger brother Johnny was completely mad, as if he didn't have an *OFF* switch. His energy levels were through the roof nearly all the time, and his mum could certainly do with a break now and again.

'Oh go on then,' she sighed, grabbing Johnny and wiping his nose with a tissue she'd kept hidden up her sleeve. 'But you both be home in time for dinner.'

'That's okay, mum,' nodded Kenny. 'I've got this.' And she disappeared down the first aisle faster than Kenny thought she would. Little Johnny just stood there grinning now, showing off the big gap in his gumsy mouth where two teeth had previously sat.

Grandpa Jock laughed at him. 'Ye're missing teeth,' he joked. 'That's whit ye get for kissing the girls.'

'That's not true,' said Johnny, looking certain and stamping his foot. 'I know that all baby teeth fall out when boys reach age five or six, no matter how many girls you kiss. My dad told me.'

'OoOoOoOooooooh,' said George and Allison together. Johnny wasn't put off.

'And I'm five,' he said to Grandpa Jock with a firm nod of his head. 'How old are you then?'

Grandpa Jock smiled, lifting his arm and leaning on the display of chocolate spread jars. 'In my thirty-two years *on this planet*, I have learned that it's okay to lie about your age.'

'What does he mean on this planet?' whispered Kenny, at the same time as Allison said,

'And he's certainly not thirty-two. Nobody should tell

lies, Mr Jock,' gasped Allison. 'You're not thirty-two. Is he, George?' But George was too busy listening to Johnny's next question.

'Do you wee into a plastic bag?' asked Johnny, with a very serious face.

'Not usually,' laughed Grandpa Jock. 'Maybe once, but that was a long journey. Why do ye ask, wee man?'

'Well, I went to visit my Gramps in hospital once, and he had a plastic bag and a tube that he wee'd into. Maybe all old people do.' Johnny's red eyebrows knitted together as he thought about the problem. 'It might save people time if we all carried plastic bags around ... like dog owners do.'

'Okay, Johnny-boy, that'll do,' said Kenny taking his brother by the hand. 'Enough already.'

But before Kenny could drag Johnny away from any more embarrassing questions, a small, angry man in a suit came stomping into the shop. He threw his leather briefcase behind the checkout counter and marched towards the end of the aisle.

'I don't pay you to chat, old fella,' snapped the small man. 'Less bleating, more greeting!'

'Just talking to a few younger customers, boss.' Grandpa Jock's face was solid, not blinking, not smiling, just set firmly. George could feel a hint of annoyance in his voice.

'Younger customers do not have enough money to spend the kind of money I want my customers to spend,' the angry guy growled. 'Children are a waste of time, old man. Where's Glen anyway?'

'Glen's finished for the day, Mr Spender,' Grandpa Jock replied. George could see a cheeky glint in his eye, whilst Allison and Kenny exchanged glances again.

'What! We have a big television advert being filmed here live, yes *LIVE* here in the store on Saturday, and I want the place spotless,' ranted Mr Spender, pointing to the big plastic bucket at the door. 'If you've got time to lean, you've got time to clean, old man. Get that bin scrubbed.'

'But I'm the Meeter and Greeter, boss,' Grandpa Jock replied quietly. 'My job is to meet and greet customers, not clean.'

'YOUR JOB IS TO DO WHATEVER I TELL YOU TO DO!' barked Mr Spender, little bits of spittle flying out of his mouth.

'Yes, boss,' grimaced Grandpa Jock. 'Ah'll go and fetch cleaning spray and a cloth, shall I?' And he sauntered off slower than George had ever seen him move.

'And you lot,' spat Mr Spender, turning to the four children. 'Buy something or get out. And no thieving. We've got cameras to catch your sticky fingers.' And the angriest little man in the world turned and marched up the next aisle, shouting more instructions at any other staff member he could find.

'Mr Spender,' gasped Allison. 'That's Jude's dad!'

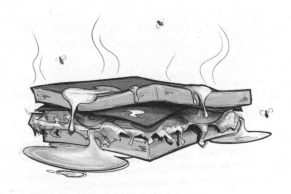

PHANTOM ERASER

DIARY UPDATE...

Met the nastiest little man in the world today. He wasn't much taller than me but he felt like he needed to be _louder_ than everyone else. I can understand why Mr Jock hates his job so much.

MR JOCK

He didn't even call Mr Jock by his name, just called him 'old man' and 'old fella' all the time. How rude! George said that Mr Jock told him that his boss didn't even bother to learn people's names, as most people didn't stay working in the shop very long. I know what he means.

SO! MANY! QUESTIONS!

And then we had Kenny's little brother with us. My goodness, he is hard work. I don't think I've ever met a kid that can ask as many questions as that wee guy... oh no, Mr Jock's Scottish accent is rubbing off on me too.

Johnny is a funny wee chap, always fidgeting and touching things. We had to get him out the shop pretty fast because we thought he would wreck one of the display stands. And that might get Mr Jock into even more trouble, so we took him to the park Kenny was a bit miffed because he didn't get his donuts but I think he'll need to watch his tummy if he keeps eating like that.

A List of Johnny's Questions

(or at least the ones I can remember)

ME!

1 WOULD YOU RATHER FIGHT A TIGER-SIZED HAMSTER OR 100 HAMSTER- SIZED TIGERS?
2 WHY HAS THAT LADY GOT A BIG BOTTOM?
3 CAN WE ASK MUM FOR A HAMSTER WHEN WE GET HOME?
4 DO YOU HAVE A HAMSTER, ALLISON?
5 WHO WIN A FIGHT BETWEEN PAW PATROL AND BATMAN?
6 DO YOU HAVE A HAMSTER, GEORGE?
7 CAN YOU MAKE A NOISE LIKE A LASER? ← SO. ANNOYING...
8 WHY DON'T YOU LIKE HAMSTERS, GEORGE?

GROSS!!!

9 HAVE YOU EVER EATEN YOUR OWN EARWAX, ALLISON? (NO!) KENNY HAS!
10 IF MY MUM SAID I COULDN'T RUN AROUND THE GARDEN WITH NO CLOTHES ON, DO YOU THINK I COULD JUST WALK INSTEAD?
11 WERE THERE ANY DINOSAURS WHEN MR JOCK WAS LITTLE?
12 DO YOU BELIEVE IN GHOSTS?
13 DO YOU BELIEVE IN MONSTERS, ALLISON? (I'M STARTING TO, JOHNNY!)
14 WHAT ABOUT THE MONSTER UNDER YOUR BED? (WEIRDO!)

As Mr Jock would say, he really is a Little Johnny Squeaker!

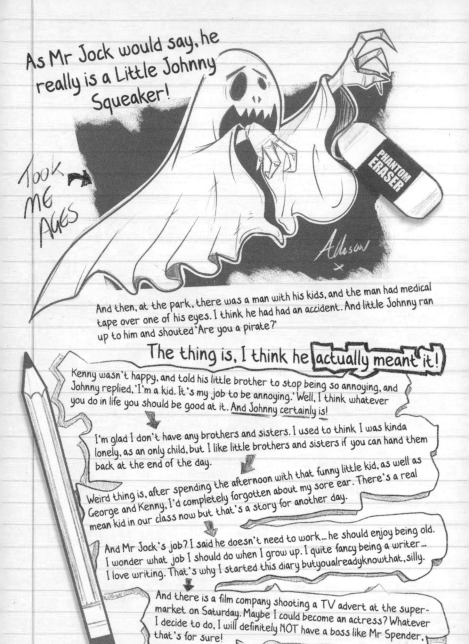

Took
ME
AGES →

PHANTOM ERASER

Allison x

And then, at the park, there was a man with his kids, and the man had medical tape over one of his eyes. I think he had had an accident. And little Johnny ran up to him and shouted 'Are you a pirate?'

The thing is, I think he actually meant it!

Kenny wasn't happy, and told his little brother to stop being so annoying, and Johnny replied, 'I'm a kid. It's my job to be annoying.' Well, I think whatever you do in life you should be good at it. And Johnny certainly is!

I'm glad I don't have any brothers and sisters. I used to think I was kinda lonely, as an only child, but I like little brothers and sisters if you can hand them back at the end of the day.

Weird thing is, after spending the afternoon with that funny little kid, as well as George and Kenny, I'd completely forgotten about my sore ear. There's a real mean kid in our class now but that's a story for another day.

And Mr Jock's job? I said he doesn't need to work... he should enjoy being old. I wonder what job I should do when I grow up. I quite fancy being a writer... I love writing. That's why I started this diary butyoualreadyknowthat, silly.

And there is a film company shooting a TV advert at the super-market on Saturday. Maybe I could become an actress? Whatever I decide to do, I will definitely NOT have a boss like Mr Spender, that's for sure!

Chapter Fifteen - A New Day

Miss Mack's classroom was very quiet the next day. It was Friday morning, and Jude had been first to arrive, as well as first back into the class after break. He had sat down at his desk without making a sound. Each time Miss Mack had given him a firm stare over her glasses but Jude just smiled sheepishly and started to read his book.

Shortly afterwards, the other pupils filed in quietly after break-time too, despite the excitement they'd been having in the playground just moments before. They had been giggling and sharing their own thoughts about Poop-Gate, as it was now called, from the day before. *Had he really poo'd himself? Was it actually chocolate? Why is it called Poop-Gate?*

George had to point out that all grown-ups now use the suffix -Gate with any exciting story these days. There had been *Party-Gate*, and *Spy-Gate* and even *Horse-Gate* in the news recently. It all started in America when some men sneaked into an office complex to steal stuff to help the President, but this happened over fifty years ago. The office complex was called the Watergate.

'And now everything is something -*Gate*,' announced George. 'This time, Poop-Gate works for me.'

'Well done, George. That was very *Jock-esque*,' giggled Kenny, nudging George in the ribs.

'I can't help it if I pick up things, especially from Grandpa Jock,' replied George, lowering his voice as the line of pupils entered the classroom. Jude was sitting there at his desk, bolt upright but head down in his book, almost challenging any one of them to snigger.

'Right, story books out,' announced Miss Mack. 'Literacy lessons again, and we shall continue with *Aesop's Fables*.'

Allison sat upright, her head snapping back. She yanked

the drawer out from under the table and searched frantically for her story book. She'd loved last week's lesson about *The Fox and The Grapes*, and how the fox failed to reach the grapes and went away feeling very bitter about it. George and Kenny were much slower in reaching for their books, not even pulling the drawer out, but just rummaging around beneath the desk.

'If you remember,' said Miss Mack in a loud clear voice. 'We are studying a series of stories collected under the name *Aesop's Fables*. Aesop was a slave and storyteller, who was believed to have lived in ancient Greece around the 6th Century BC.'

'He didn't write the stories though, did he, Miss?' Allison's hand had shot up but she didn't wait to be asked.

'That's correct, Allison,' nodded Miss Mack. 'At that time, the stories were passed on by word of mouth, and only written down three hundred years after Aesop's time. Perhaps his most famous tales would be *The Boy Who Cried Wolf* and *The Goose That Laid The Golden Egg*.'

'Will we be reading one of those stories today, Miss?' blurted Allison, flicking through her book to find the right page first.

'Not today, Allison. Today we will be looking at *The Boy And The Nettle*.' And Miss Mack turned to a page in her book that had been marked with a bright yellow post-it note.

She started reading about a boy who had been playing out in the fields when he spied a large patch of berries growing in a hedgerow. He thought about how tasty the berries would be, so he gently reached in to pick them when his hand was stung by a nettle. He jumped back as his hand began to burn, red welts appearing on his skin. The boy ran to tell his mother, and between sobs he said "I only touched it ever so lightly, mother."

At this point, Miss Mack held the book up and declared in

a sing-song voice...

'And his mother replied,

"Gently touch a nettle and it'll sting you for your pains.
Grasp it as a lad of mettle and soft as silk remains."'

Allison almost burst into a round of applause, she was so delighted. There was always something special about story time. George and Kenny just looked at each other.

'What do you think the story is trying to tell us?' asked Miss Mack, closing the book and looking around the class.

Kenny thrust up his hand. 'Don't touch jaggy nettles!' he shouted.

'Not quite, Kenny,' replied Miss Mack, patiently. 'The boy's mother said you could grasp the nettle if you did it firmly.'

Allison raised her hand a little more gingerly this time, unsure of her answer. 'Does it mean that whatever you do, do with all your might? You know, try your best.'

'Excellent, Allison,' yelped Miss Mack, clapping her hands together. 'Whatever you do, do your best. A wonderful lesson in life, children, don't you think?'

A few children bobbed their heads up and down silently. Allison nodded her head furiously but Jude Spender just smiled.

'Now, after lunch we are going to write our own fables,' said Miss Mack. 'You can think of a lesson you'd like people to learn, perhaps include an animal like a fox or a dog to be the main character and a problem those characters will face.'

Allison nodded again. George and Kenny nudged each other, grinning.

But Jude Spender just smiled quietly, which was worrying.

Editor's note

I'd just like to point out that...

Illustrator's note

Hope you are not going to start ranting like the last time.

Editor's note

Well, I believe that children are our future. Teach them well, and ...

Illustrator's note

Oh no, he's gonna start singing!

Editor's note

I'm just saying... my children are all grown up and have gone to university, and have got themselves good jobs, so ...

Illustrator's note

So, what? Do you want a sticker too?

Editor's note

No, I am merely sharing some of my wisdom with the young readers here ... but I must say those stickers are pretty cool.

Illustrator's note

Like this one here?

!!!EXCITING!!! YES

Miss Mack has just told us that we will be writing our own fables this afternoon! I am so excited that I can't even eat my lunch (cheese and pickle sandwiches, with a packet of crisps and an apple - thanks mum).

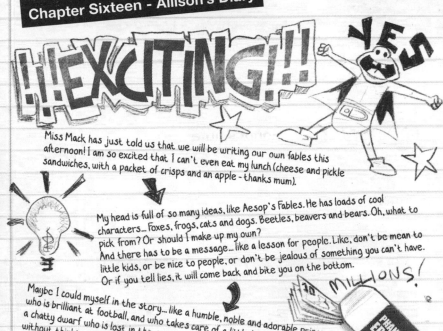

My head is full of so many ideas, like Aesop's Fables. He has loads of cool characters... Foxes, frogs, cats and dogs. Beetles, beavers and bears. Oh, what to pick from? Or should I make up my own?

And there has to be a message... like a lesson for people. Like, don't be mean to little kids, or be nice to people, or don't be jealous of something you can't have. Or if you tell lies, it will come back and bite you on the bottom.

Maybe I could myself in the story... like a humble, noble and adorable princess, who is brilliant at football, and who takes care of a little lamb lost in the field, or a chatty dwarf who is lost in the supermarket. Or a pirate who says things without thinking, and upsets people without realising.

And I should get story published too. I could earn a million pounds (Note to self - stay humble, Allison). Or a fable about an author who has a rags-to-riches live, made a million pounds and then forgot about all the hard work that went into story-writing in the early days.

Or maybe a fable about a celebrity singer who thinks they can write children's books (because all famous people think they can write children's books these days) and they stop singing, and write a book that is totally rubbish and nobody buys the book BUT the singer can't go back to their singing career because their voice has been trapped inside their book. (Note to self - breathe, Allison, breathe... and punctuate your sentences!)

PRINCESS LEAGUE ?

I just can't make up my mind.... there's so much to choose from. I will just need to slow down, take my time and plan my story properly.

Oh no, it's nearly time to head back to school, and I haven't even started my lunch yet. No time now... I'll just have to go hungry.

That's it! I'm definitely becoming an author now!

Chapter Seventeen - Hungry?

Allison had thrown her diary and her pencil into her bag, and was skipping furiously back to school. Her long, dark ponytail was bouncing along behind her. Allison liked to skip, she thought it was more graceful than running. She couldn't understand why more adults didn't skip themselves. It was as if they'd completely forgotten about one of the simple joys of childhood.

She rounded the corner at the edge of the school lane, and braked sharply. George and Kenny were standing there just before the school gates, next to the fence, shuffling their feet and whispering. Allison nearly collided with them.

'Whoa! Slow that train, Noodle-brain. What's the rush?' George looked surprised at her hurry to get back to school.

'Yeah, what he said, Noodle-head,' added Kenny. 'The bell won't go for another five minutes.'

'I just like to be organised,' replied Allison, ignoring the *Noodle* comments. 'Anyway, what are you two up to?'

'Kenny was just telling about his fable. It's brilliant,' laughed George, throwing his head back.

'Homework, Kenny? That's not like you,' teased Allison.

'Well, what can I say? When inspiration strikes, you just have to go with it.' Kenny shrugged and pushed his lip out, showing his false modesty. 'I mean, during lunch break there, I was sitting on the toilet reading a book...'

'As you do,' added George.

'Yes, as I do, George. Quite frequently,' Kenny added with a grin. Reading on the toilet was one of his favourite hobbies. He enjoyed the peace and quiet in there, and often his legs would go numb as he became lost in the pages of whatever novel or a comic-book he'd been reading.

'Anyway, today I was reading a brilliant book called *Timewarp Trouser Trumpets*,' he winked at George. 'And an idea struck me. The title, *Timewarp Trouser Trumpets*, Tee Tee Tee is an alliteration, when the words start with the same sound in the same sentence.'

'Yeah, we know what an alliteration is,' said Allison, impatiently. 'Miss Mack spoke about them last term.'

'So I came up with my own alliteration story.' Kenny spread his hands out wide, as if revealing his great secret.

'Tell her the title, Kenny,' nodded George, almost as excited as his pal. 'Go on, tell her. Wait till you hear this, Allison.'

Kenny paused for dramatic effect, took a deep breath, then announced,

'*Krazy Krayon Kenny and his Karate Kicking Kangaroo!* With all the words starting with K,' he declared, looking smug. 'I'll be the star in my story, and I reckon I can spell *crazy* and *crayon* with a special K because that's my superhero name.'

'And it's like your favourite donuts,' added George. 'Krispy Kreme!' Kenny nodded, licking his lips. *Nom, nom, nom.*

'So what's it about?' asked Allison, not quite sure if she wanted to know the answer. At that moment, her tummy growled, as she thought about the donuts.

'Well,' shrugged Kenny. 'I hadn't really thought about it much. I was kinda hoping that the title spoke for itself. It's about a kangaroo that goes around...'

'Karate kicking people, perhaps?' Allison threw this in quickly, and raised one of her eyebrows.

'Yeah, obviously,' Kenny replied, with a puzzled look on his face. 'But I haven't, you know, worked out all the details yet.'

'And wait until you hear mine, Allison.' George was also bursting to share his story. Allison wanted to roll her eyes but didn't want to appear rude. She took a deep breath.

'Go on then,' sighed Allison, again not sure if she wanted to hear this either. But Kenny did. He hadn't heard George's story idea yet and was hoping his friend had come up with a cracker, or perhaps even a *kracker*.

'We've been reading *Aesop's Fables* in class, right? And our stories can have animals or people or objects, as long as our fable has a message to it, yeah?' said George, building up to his big reveal. He always seemed to enjoy these moments.

'The title of my story is...' George paused, hoping to add to the drama, as Kenny began drumming his hands on the fence behind them. *These two just feed off each other*, thought Allison, straight away regretting any thoughts about feeding. Her tummy grumbled again.

'The Boiled Egg and the Donkey!' declared George, wiggling his eyebrows.

'Awesome,' yelled Kenny.

'Rubbish,' said Allison.

'That's a bit harsh,' replied George, somewhat deflated.

'Sorry, George, but I think I've heard this story before. It's the same as your grandpa's,' said Allison, trying to soften her blow. 'What's the message in your fable?'

'Don't stick hot boiled eggs up donkeys' bottoms, obviously!' shouted Kenny with a smile, thinking back to Grandpa Jock's story.

'Well, yeah, kind of,' paused George, trying to come up with something smarter on the spot. He hadn't really

thought his story through either. 'But more about, well, erm, thinking about the after-effects of your actions.'

Allison nodded. 'Aaaah I see,' she said. 'Like, doing something without thinking about what might happen next? You know, *consequences*.'

George was nodding too. 'That's the word I was looking for!' he yelled, snapping his fingers.

Kenny's eyes were sparkling. 'Like there…' He pointed to the gap at the end of the metal railings. 'Remember that time when I pushed my head through the bars of this fence, and I couldn't pull my head out because my ears were stuck.'

'And the fire brigade had to come and cut you free,' giggled George, thinking back.

'Yeah, I should've thought that one through really,' smiled Kenny.

Editor's note

Readers, please do not stick your heads through the railings of a fence. You might get stuck.

Author's note

No, don't do that. Just tell your little brother to do it instead. He's smaller than you.

Illustrator's note

NO!!!!!! He's kidding, readers!!! Nobody stick their heads between the bars of a fence. Ever!

Author's note
Spoilsport!

Allison chuckled when Kenny said 'that ONE' because she could think of several other incidents that he hadn't thought through properly. Before she could offer up a suggestion, the bell rang. Lunchtime was over!

Yeah, lunchtime was over, and her stomach growled again. She should've eaten something, even if she wanted to become a poor, starving author before she made her millions. All this talk about donuts, noodles and boiled eggs had made her feel even hungrier. She even thought she could be tempted to eat a boiled egg that *had* come out of a donkey's bottom, as long as she washed her hands after taking the shell off. *Urgh*, Allison gagged.

As they all walked through the school gates, George snuck up to her from behind.

'Here, you should eat this,' whispered George, handing her a cereal bar. 'I was saving it for later but sounds like you need it more than I do.'

Chapter Eighteen - Jaggies

Allison was wiping the crumbs from around the edges of her mouth as they all entered the classroom. She ducked her head down behind George and Kenny, so that Miss Mack couldn't see she was still eating, and swallowed her final mouthful. That cereal bar had been tasty, and thankfully, her tummy had stopped grumbling.

The boys noticed that Jude was sitting politely at his desk again, hands together, fingers folded, with his usual smug sneer across his face. He was there even before Miss Mack had come back from the staffroom, which was odd. Had Jude turned over a new leaf?

George didn't have time to think about it by the time he sat down at his desk. Miss Mack started to recap the lesson from before lunch, and invited a few children to share their ideas about the fables they were going to write.

Some of the storylines had clearly been stolen from movies, such as the little girl who had been whisked away from her house by a tornado, and over the rainbow where she met a scarecrow, a robot and a tiger. Miss Mack had said that the moral of the story, *there's no place like home*, was a good one but she wanted more originality. George thought that nobody, except Allison and Kenny, would ever have heard of his story before.

Miss Mack also enjoyed one idea from the girl who sat next to Allison. Her story was all about a little baby penguin who had lost its mummy and daddy in a snow storm, and every time it went off to find them, the little penguin slipped and fell over. The ice was so slippery, and the baby penguin had only just learned to walk. Time and time again the fluffy chick fell on its bottom, and over and over again the little penguin picked itself up and tried to waddle off. Eventually, the chick found its mummy and daddy, who had been sick with worry.

The moral of her story was *never give up*, and Allison nodded her approval. She liked fluffy little penguins. But Kenny just giggled when the girl said 'bottom'.

'Alright, boys and girls,' announced Miss Mack. 'Your ideas are wonderful, and I'm delighted to hear that most of you have clearly put a lot of thought into them.' At this point, she looked across to Kenny with a raised eyebrow.

At first, Kenny had decided that the moral of his story was *Don't teach your kangaroo karate or go around kicking people* but Miss Mack suggested that he give his story some more thought.

'So, quickly and quietly, can you reach into your drawers and bring out your literacy jotters?' Miss Mack put this out as a question but in truth it was really an instruction, and her pupils didn't need telling twice. As one, they all slipped their hands beneath their desks, Allison faster than most others. It was at that point she screamed!

George and Kenny yelped loudly too, and whipped their hands back from out of their desk drawers. Their fingers were covered with angry, red welts, and the boys could feel them throbbing. Allison cried out again, as she held up her arms, frightened to touch anything. A burning sensation was spreading across her skin, and she could see a group of little needles sticking out from the red rashes on the back of her hands.

Miss Mack ran over to where Allison was sitting, and saw her hands swelling. She turned to see George and Kenny holding their arms up too, and then she looked underneath Allison's desk.

The space beneath had been filled with a jungle of green leaves; the whole area between the desk and the drawer contents bursting out with stinging nettles.

Miss Mack shouted, 'Don't itch! Don't scratch! You'll only make it worse. Let's get you three to the medical room.' There was an urgency in her voice, as she helped Allison out of her chair. Allison didn't want to touch anything with her aching fingers, so Miss Mack reached for the handle of the classroom door and pulled. George and Kenny were struggling out of their chairs too, as Miss Mack yelled back across…

'Follow us this way, boys. I'll get the doors.' And she eased Allison out of the classroom and into the corridor. The boys had squeezed out from behind their double desk, and were shuffling towards the front of the class.

'I dunno which one of you two spread the chocolate on my chair,' hissed Jude Spender, as they walked by. 'So I had to get you both! Say anything to anyone, and you're dead meat.'

George and Kenny swapped glances, gulped, and shambled faster out of the classroom.

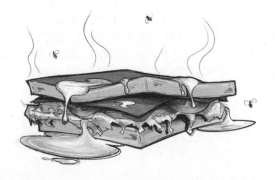

Chapter Nineteen - Poo Sticks

Washed up, stingers removed and ice patches applied, George, Allison and Kenny spent the rest of the afternoon in the medical room feeling sorry for themselves. They knew who had planted the nettles in their desks but were feeling powerless to do anything about it.

'We should get our own back on Jude. I've had enough of his nonsense,' growled Kenny. 'First, he stands on George's head at the football match, then he attacks you in the classroom, Allison. Now he's got us all jaggied and stung. My hands are throbbing!'

'I think we would be opening a cans of worms there, Kenny,' replied Allison. 'It might be wiser to turn the other cheek.'

Kenny's face was genuinely shocked. 'The other cheek?' he gasped. 'I'm not baring my bum to Jude Spender.'

'Not that kind of cheek, Kenny,' groaned Allison. Was this boy for real? 'I just meant that we forgive and forget. Move on.'

George thought for a second or two, then shook his head. 'Don't you remember, Allison, That fable about the farmer and the snake?' Allison nodded slowly but Kenny just shook his head. Things took a while to sink into his head sometimes.

'Oh yeah,' said Allison softly. 'Injuries may be forgiven, but never forgotten.'

'And my Grandpa Jock told me once that before someone seeks revenge, they first need to dig two graves.'

'We can't kill him!' squealed Kenny, the colour draining from his face. 'That would be so wrong... and I don't wanna go to jail!'

'Of course not,' Allison said sharply. 'It's just an old saying. It means that if we hurt Jude somehow, we may end up hurting ourselves too. We should think about the consequences of our actions. Like the moral in George's story.'

'What? My donkey and his boiled egg?' George eyes widened as he realised for the first time his story might have some merit. It was like searching the biscuit barrel for the last digestive but finding a chocolate hob-bob instead! *Result!* he thought to himself. If Allison thinks his idea is a good one, then Miss Mack would love it.

'We should visit my Grandpa Jock after school,' urged George. 'He's always got good biscuits. I mean, ideas. He's always got good ideas.'

'Maybe he'll have good donuts this time too,' moaned Kenny.

Unbelievably, Grandpa Jock did have donuts in his cupboard this time. And more digestives. And even chocolate hob-bobs. As George's mum and dad worked long, long hours, the school had Grandpa Jock's telephone number as his emergency contact, and they'd called him to say about the nettle stings. Grandpa Jock figured that although their hands had been patched up they'd still be sore, so biscuits, donuts and hot chocolate might help take the children's minds off the pain.

So he'd ran down to All-Days (well, as fast as his old-geezer-legs could carry him), and avoided his boss, Mr Spender, who was walking around the shop with his briefcase, trying to seem important and shouting at a couple of staff members in the pasta aisle. Grandpa Jock made it safely into the biscuit section and chuckled when he remembered he wasn't supposed to say *staff members* any more because supermarkets want their staff to be called *colleagues* now because it was lighter, and fluffier, and made people feel *part of the team*, instead of the underpaid, badly treated serfs that they actually are.

He'd grabbed an armful of the tastiest treats he could find, (including that new chocolate spread that was on offer) paid for them (obviously) and ran home, just in time to meet George, Kenny, Allison *and* his postman all standing at his back door.

'Hey, Frank,' he shouted. 'How ya doing?'

'I'm good, Jock, thanks. Parcel for you here though. It's that time again,' laughed Frank the postman, in the cheeriest voice Allison had ever heard. 'Too big to fit in your letterbox!'

Frank the postman chuckled, handed the large brown package to George with a wink, and then tootled off up the street, humming a happy, little tune.

'What's that, Grandpa?' asked George, as Grandpa Jock snatched the parcel out of George's still-throbbing hands, and threw it onto the orange worktop in the kitchen.

'Ah well, I wuz gonna say "never you mind" but you'll find oot one day,' sighed the old Scotman. 'It's ma poop-on-a-paddle pack.'

'Poop-on-a-paddle?' yelled all three children at once.

'Okay, okay. Let me show ye,' said Grandpa Jock, ripping open the package and emptying out a letter, some labels, a tube and what looked like a plastic lollipop stick.

'Right, everybody poops, yeah?' It was more of a statement, less of a question. 'And when people get older, everybody should check their poop. I mean, that Dame Debra bowel babe wuz brilliant, and even the health service want to check your poop nowadays, just to make sure that people are staying healthy.'

'Urgh,' gagged Allison. 'You mean doctors look at your poo?!'

'Yeah, every two years,' nodded Grandpa Jock. 'It wuz a shock to me too. I didn't even know aboot this stuff. The health service send ye a kit like this on your 50th birthday, actually on yer birthday, like a wee present.' He pointed down at the contents of the parcel.

'And you check your own poo, Mr Jock?' Kenny was staring in amazement at the collection of odd-shaped bits of plastic, like the little toys that come out of small chocolate eggs, only kinder.

'Well naw, Kenny. Ah don't check ma own poo.' Grandpa Jock picked up the lollipop stick and tube. 'Ye squeeze a wee turd out into the toilet. Ye stab it with this stick, pop the poop stick into the tube. Then post the poop tube back to the doctor's. They test it, and hopefully, send you back the *All Clear!* Does that make sense?'

'Just one thing, Mr Jock,' said Allison, screwing her face up. 'What's a turd?'

Grandpa Jock glanced around suspiciously, just in case someone might be listening, then whispered, 'It's a cheeky wee word for poo. No big deal. There's a lot more wrong with this world than a wee turd.'

'And you send it away in the post?' asked George. 'So why is your postman always looking so happy when he has to deliver poo-sticks to doctors? At any moment, his bag might be full of poo!'

Editor's note

Stuart, you can't use rude words like 'turd'. We'll get complaints.

Author's note

Well, we'll tell them to just stop being snowflakes. Anyway, it's not rude, Ed. A little bit cheeky but not rude. See...

Dictionary Definition

Turd: *t-uh-rd - noun, slang. Definition a piece of poop. Mild expletive, not a swear word, merely impolite and very informal. Only for use amongst friends. Not for use in schools or in front of parents, teachers and/or significant adults.*

Chapter Twenty - Grasping Nettles

Grandpa Jock boiled the kettle and made each of the children a steaming mug of hot chocolate, each one with fluffy marshmallows floating around on the top. The kids eyed their mugs carefully, not really wanting to pick them up with their swollen fingers. Kenny had been scratching at his hands, his arms *and* his armpits since they'd arrived.

The old Scotsman reached into his bag of goodies, pulled out a box of paper straws, popped the lid and slipped a straw into each mug. He'd thought of everything.

'Up there for thinking, down there for dancin', said the old geezer, with a shoogly little dance on his kitchen floor. 'Noo, let's see those fingers.'

George, Allison and Kenny all held out their hands, trying to show off who had the worst of the stings, burns and welts. Their skin was quite swollen and border-line infected but nothing that a few biscuits and donuts couldn't solve.

'Ah'll even let ye spread some of that new chocolate stuff all over yer donut, Kenny, eh? Would that help?' Grandpa Jock winked, and Kenny grinned, stopped scratching under his arm-pits and ripped at the plastic covering on the box of donuts.

At least he's stopped picking his nose, thought Allison *but he's itching far more than he should be. My hands aren't that sore.* Allison couldn't leave it. She had to ask.

'Kenny,' she said. 'Why do you keep scratching yourself?'

'Because I'm the only one who knows where the itch is!' and Kenny shrugged, stating the obvious.

'Aye, Jaggy nettles can be sore for a couple of hours but after that, ye'll be fine,' confirmed Grandpa Jock confidently. 'In the olden days, the Romans, who weren't used to British wintertime, would rub nettles onto their legs to keep warm.'

The youngsters winced together but Grandpa Jock only laughed. 'Scottish people too, back in the olden days. See, if ye've only got a kilt on, and it starts to snow, the burn from some stinging nettles can fair put a heat in ye.'

He went on, 'And, ah don't know if this is true but, maybe as a dare, people would wipe their bottoms with jaggy nettles. Ye know, nature's toilet paper!'

George and Kenny started sniggering, and even Allison cracked a smile, thinking about the consequences.

'There wuz an old saying, back in the day,' Grandpa Jock thought out loud. 'It was when I was in Transylvania hunting vampires... let me think noo.'

Allison's eyes widened, and she stared across at George. Had he really been hunting vampires? Nobody really knew that much about Grandpa Jock's adventures in his younger days but hunting vampires? Still, nobody would put it past him.

'That's it,' he said with a jump, snapping his bony old fingers. *'The lightning bolt never strikes the nettles,* or something like that. Sounds better in Romanian but it means that the devil looks after his own, or bad people always escape trouble.'

'I know exactly what you mean, Mr Jock,' announced Allison. 'I have always said that stinging nettles were evil.'

'But bad people shouldn't escape trouble,' said Kenny. 'They should get what's coming to them.'

'Aye, ye may have a point there, lad,' Grandpa Jock nodded. 'There is another old phrase that I quite like *Grasp the nettle!* It means take the bull by the horns, or tackle some difficulty, be firm aboot stuff.'

'Are you going to take the bull by the horns with old Mr Spender then?' asked Allison, with a sly smile.

'Ah jist might do, lassie.' Grandpa Jock's eyes narrowed, and a cheeky little grin leaked out from underneath his moustache. 'Are ye gonna grasp the nettle with young Jude then, the three of youse?'

'I think I may just have a plan, Grandpa.'

'*Nettle-esque*, young man?' said Grandpa Jock smiling.

Chapter Twenty One - SaTURDay

Like most old people, Grandpa Jock woke up early each morning.

Most old people tend to go to their beds early too, like 9pm early, wake up after a couple of hours to go for a wee, make a cup of tea, then pad around their houses looking for little jobs to do at one o'clock in the morning. Often, old people might walk into one room and forget what they went in there for. Then they go back to bed. By five o'clock each morning it would be time for another wee, another cup of tea, and a little cat-nap in front of the TV. Not Grandpa Jock.

When Grandpa Jock woke up (at 5am, not the 1am wake-up for a wee time) he was always an excited ball of energy. He never knew what adventures would lie ahead of him each day. On his 60th birthday, Grandpa Jock realised that he was well into the final quarter of his life, so he worked out how many days he had left to live, roughly speaking. Just over five thousand, if he was lucky.

Five thousand might sound like a lot but those days can tick away faster than the hands of a clock, if you're not careful.

Editor's note

Kids, don't worry too much about numbers like that. You've all probably got at least twenty-five thousand days left. Well, boys do. Girls have got an extra 2,000 days because they look after themselves properly. Use your days well. Have fun, laugh a lot, hug your friends, love yourself, spend less time on your phone, try new things, be kind to people and animals, enjoy life...

Illustrator's note

Ed, ed, ed, ED, ED, ED ED! You're getting carried away again. Calm down, man!

Grandpa Jock reckoned he gone passed his sell-by date a few years ago but he could never be sure. Living life to its fullest meant not worrying too much about birthday candles, so he didn't. He could've checked his birth certificate or one of his old passports but what would that prove? His age, sure, but what would it matter? Grandpa Jock thought that age was just a number.

Time was a-wasting and there was fun to be had.

By six o'clock each morning Grandpa Jock would usually be down by the pond, feeding the ducks. He never threw bread, instead carrying a little bag of peas, sweetcorn and seeds to the edge of the water, where he would enjoy watching the ducks living their best life, racing in to catch the little snacks. By eight o'clock, he'd be having a wee cup of tea with his friends at the cafe … but not today. Grandpa Jock had headed for All-Days.

Not that he was working today. Grandpa Jock was only part-time, never worked weekends, and only did it because he enjoyed meeting people. Today, there was something else going on.

The road leading out of Little Pumpington was a downward slope. It ran downhill towards the All-Days superstore, which had been built at the edge of town. *To make people drive further, and need to fill up with more fuel at their petrol station* Grandpa Jock always thought.

Today though, he stopped at the top of the hill and hissed under his breath. *'Shizzle Sticks!'* he cursed.

Somebody, some careless waster, had dumped an All-Days shopping trolley in the bushes at the side of the road. Glen the trolley boy never came this far up, so there was a good chance that the trolley would lie there and rust, looking all ugly and spoiling the scenery. So, Grandpa Jock, being a good citizen, pulled the trolley out of the bushes with every intention of wheeling it back to the store.

However, Grandpa Jock, being a big kid at heart, with the mental age of a ten year old, decided to climb into the trolley and point it downhill towards the car park. *What a great idea*, he thought.

At least, it seemed like a great idea at the time. As he hurtled down the path, picking up speed all the time, it didn't seem like such a good idea now. Getting started was easy; gravity took care of that. Stopping was an after-thought, and it only occurred to him as the wind whipped at his moustache and the bouncing trolley rattled his false teeth around his mouth. He liked these false teeth too, very comfy, and certainly didn't want to break them with a crash into a trolley-bay, or worse!

The trolley bumped off the path and onto the road. *Not a good idea, Jock*, he thought to himself, as the danger of the situation became clear. A small red car had to swerve to avoid hitting him. The car then bumped up and over the mini-roundabout in the middle of the road and disappeared down towards the canal.

'Sorry missus,' muttered Grandpa Jock, under his breath. 'Poor woman didn't even have time to toot her horn at me.'

The trolley trundled on, bumping off the road now and down into the car park. As he zipped passed the first trolley-bay, Grandpa Jock screamed 'LOOK OUT!!!' towards the parked cars and a large van parked in the corner. This was not going to be pretty.

The group of people shuffling around beside the parked cars had heard the rumblings of the runaway trolley, and the old man screaming at the top of his voice, and had all dived for safety.

But, as if by some miracle, a weird kind of superhero in a long, green cape leapt from behind the trolley-bay, grabbed the handle bar and dug his heels into the tarmac. Sparks flew from his boots, as the trolley slowed to a halt.

'Ya beauty!' yelled Grandpa Jock, hopping out of the trolley. 'You're ma hero, Glen!'

Glen Pearce was a spotty teenager, with lanky hair and trousers that were a tad too short for his legs. He shuffled his feet, as his face turned red, embarrassed and unused to praise. Glen mumbled, 'No problem, Mr Jock. You were out of control there.'

'Well, ye saved me and ma teeth, young man!' gushed Grandpa Jock. 'Thank you, and ah'll sort ye out with a wee bonus later.' The old Scotsman winked. 'The bacon butties are on me!'

Glen wasn't really wearing a superhero's cape but he never buttoned up the front of his green overall, even though Mr Spender always told him to, shouting about it most of the time. Glen liked the way his overall flew out behind him when he ran with a line of trolleys, *superhero-esque*.

'I recognise that accent,' came a posh, clipped voice from behind the van. 'Mr Jonathon 'Jock' Hansen, the prancing, pink pensioner, if I am not mistaken.'

Grandpa Jock turned and laughed. He'd enjoyed a tiny flicker of fame a few years ago, as he held a one-man protest against a fast-food company that put poo in their burgers. He'd dyed his hair pink and wore a pink toga, as he danced on the roof of the burger shop. His protest had been filmed and the video went viral. The director was a frightfully nice chap called Tarquin Lucius-Superbus.

'TARQUIN!' Grandpa Jock yelled, throwing up his arms. 'How ye daein', laddie?'*

Editor's note

*You should've read the Intro. *See Translation 1 - Introduction.*

'I am absolutely marvellous, Jock, thank you,' replied Tarquin, straightening his yellow cravat. 'Narrowly avoided being struck by a runaway shopping trolley there but delighted to see you still have your spirit, sir.'

'Whit are ye daein' here, Tarks?' asked Grandpa Jock, keen to catch up with the TV director.

'Wur daein'… ahem,' coughed Tarquin, slipping into Jock's easy Scottish dialect. 'I mean to say, we are doing a television advert here at All-Days. Filming it live, and broadcasting to millions of people on TV and across social media immediately. The wonders of technology, Jock.'

Tarquin fiddled with his cravat again, and snapped his waistcoat down tightly. The flower in his lapel buttonhole was beginning to wilt, and it was only eight o'clock in the morning. His usually beautifully coiffed hair was frazzling at the sides, and his left eye twitched now and again.

'Ye're looking a wee touch flustered, Tarks.' Grandpa Jock's eyebrows knitted together, and he pursed his lips. 'Is everything okay?'

'I am afraid not, Jock,' sighed Tarquin. 'We appear to have lost our props lady.'

Chapter Twenty Two - Sick

Inside the store, things were frantic. Grimley Spender had stashed his briefcase behind the check-out counter at the front of the shop, and was running up and down the aisles, shouting, yelling and screaming at each and every staff member he could find. He had to look hard for some of them too, especially the ones hiding in the toilets.

He had told the staff to pull forward all the products on every shelf in the store to make the shelves look full. Labels were turned to the front, no barcodes were showing and the end result was impressive. Gaps were covered up and filled in, and even if some products were missing, at least the shop *looked* good for the TV cameras. Grimley Spender knew that the All-Days big bosses would be watching his advert on television so first impressions, even if he cheated, were all that mattered.

The camera crew were setting up their equipment in the corner, running tests and keeping their heads down but still listening to the manager's constant ranting. Grimley had already told Tarquin that both he and his son Jude would be the stars of the advert, selling the product and promoting his shop at the same time. The camera crew had worked with lots of so-called 'celebrities' on all kinds of film shoots, so they'd dealt with 'difficult' performers in the past; *Divas*, Tarquin called them. Grimley Spender would need careful handling.

Now, similar to most supermarkets, the fruit and veg aisle was the first one that customers walked up. Just before the fresh produce aisle, there was a large display stand, filled to the brim with hundreds of jars of *Spr3d the Chocolate*. This was going to be the main area featured in the advert.

'PUT THAT BACK!' Grimley screamed at an old lady who had just picked up a jar of *Spr3d the Chocolate* from the display. 'That's not sale… it's for my advert. Leave it alone, and get out of this aisle,' he ranted. 'Nobody wants to see you on the telly.' The poor lady got such a fright she nearly dropped the jar, and maybe even a little bit of wee-wee slipped out, but she carefully put the jar back exactly where she found it and hurried off into the next aisle.

Managing a shop would be easy, if it wasn't for stupid customers, growled Grimley to himself, as he adjusted the jar that the lady had touched a fraction of a millimetre. He turned his head, as he heard more customers come into his shop. *What do they want now?*

It was the same two customers that he'd seen a couple of days before. Grimley had taken an instant dislike to the woman because she didn't buy very much, just a few essentials. And he certainly hated the small boy, the one in the Batman t-shirt who'd been keeping his staff members back from their work. *Yeah, the lazy, old guy*, he thought.

This time, Johnny wasn't happy. His face was pale and he was dragging his feet, despite his mum's attempts to pull him along a bit quicker.

'I feel sick,' wailed Johnny, letting his tongue loll out of the side of his mouth.

'Well, it's your own fault,' snapped Kenny's mum. 'I come downstairs on a Saturday morning, and find you up early, stuffing your face with your second big box of ChoKo-Pops! You're not supposed to eat them all at once. They're meant to last the whole week.'

Mrs Roberts was in full motherly flow now; you know,

that rant where poor exhausted mums have to pick up the pieces of whatever nonsense their children (usually boys, and often husbands too) have left in their wake. This time, Johnny had been watching cartoons and eating cereal straight out of the box with his fingers. He'd also had three chocolate biscuits, two hob-bobs and a packet of crisps before starting on the Choko-Pops.

'And you don't even wake up that early on a school day,' she went on. 'But hey, it's Saturday! Don't bother giving your mother a long lie-in. Just eat the two boxes of cereal that I'd only bought on Thursday and leave nothing for anybody else's breakfast. Selfish, Johnny, just self...'

Kenny's mum stopped in mid-sentence. Johnny's hand had slipped from hers, and he was standing facing a large basket of cauliflowers. And he was being sick!

'Bleeeeeeugghhhhhhhh!'

Johnny stopped, and gave out a short sigh of relief, followed by some breathless panting. His mum was frozen to the spot. Should she move him mid-barf? Johnny cleared his throat with a dribbly cough, and began again.

'Bleeeeeeeeeeeuuuuuuuugggggggggggghhhhhhhhh!

Bleugh, bleugh.........blah.'

A sea of sick splattered over the whole tray of cauliflowers again, and the smell was absolutely honking. None of the barf was on the floor. All of it, his entire stomach contents, all brown and chocolatey, with a few little pieces of sweetcorn thrown up for good measure, covered the vegetables. Little kids are never quite sure when puke is going to creep up on them, and that lot certainly crept up on Johnny.

'Get that disgusting child out of my shop now!' screamed Grimley Spender, panicking at the state of his store just before his big screen debut. Mrs Roberts was too busy hauling Johnny off to the toilets to argue with the manager but she wouldn't forget him.

'Glen!' cried Grimley. 'Glen, get over here now.' And the lanky shop assistant appeared round the corner at a trot.

'Take these cauliflowers through the back, wash them under the tap and get them back out here pronto!' barked Grimley, pointing at the veg. 'I don't want any wastage.'

'Urgh… but they're covered in vomit, Mr Spender,' groaned Glen, feeling his own stomach churn.

'I know they're covered in vomit, idiot. That's why I want you to clean them up,' cried Grimley. 'Filming starts in less than an hour, and I want those cauliflowers back out here on sale sharpish!'

Carefully, doing exactly as he was told, Glen picked up the basket of white, green and now brown vegetables and carried them through to the chilled produce area in the warehouse. Luckily, only a small amount of puke dripped through the basket, mainly onto Glen's shoes, but he'd still have to run a mop over the floor when he was finished.

Editor's note

Apologies again readers, for another absolutely disgusting chapter. However, Stuart assures me that back in 1986, when he worked in a supermarket, a 'cauliflower incident' just like the one above actually happened! The manager in question did not want any stock losses, so the cauliflowers were cleaned and put back out on sale.

Fortunately, that particular supermarket has since gone out of business. Well, it was bought over by a bigger supermarket, and I am sure they don't do things like that anymore.

Hopefully.

Chapter Twenty Three - Propped Up

Whilst the cauliflowers were being washed, Jude arrived at the store. His father had assured him that he was going to be the star of the new television advert, and he thought it was nothing less than he deserved.

Following in his father's footsteps, Jude marched around the store, insulting staff members, issuing instructions and barking orders. He'd watched his father behave like this before, and knew exactly how top managers acted. The staff knew who Jude was, so they weren't going to risk the wrath of Mr Spender by answering this spoiled brat back.

Tarquin had popped inside, still worried about his lack of a props lady, who hadn't been seen since she left her hotel this morning. She was vital to the success of the advert, preparing the various foods that needed spreading with **Spr3d the Chocolate**.

A large crowd was beginning to gather outside the store, as the Hot-Choc Dancers arrived in their executive tour bus. It was shiny, brown and luxurious, with red and yellow **Spr3d** logos plastered all over it. And one by one, the Hot-Choc Dancers, first girl then boy, then another girl-boy combo again, skipped off in their shiny, brown outfits, posing for selfies with people from the crowd, even posing by themselves when nobody wanted to take their photo.

'I'm not sure how we're going to do this,' moaned Kenny, standing at the back of the crowd.

'We discussed it yesterday, Kenny,' said George. 'It's all planned. The old switcheroo!'

'But what if we get caught switching? We'll be in big trouble then.'

'We're not going to get caught, Crayon,' hissed George, beginning to lose patience with his pal. 'Allison will be on the inside. We'll start the distraction and Grandpa Jock will make the switch. Easy-peasy-cheesy-sneezy!'

'But Allison's not on the inside,' argued Kenny. 'She's only there.'

Kenny pointed over towards the front doors of the shop. Allison was standing at the edge of the crowd, as the Hot-Choc Dancers were still skipping and prancing into the supermarket. There were four security guards positioned at either side of the sliding doors, holding them open and allowing the dancers to slowly make their way into the store.

On the other side of the doors, Kenny could just about make out the gleam of a baldy head and the flash of a fiery, ginger moustache. Grandpa Jock had whipped out his comb and paper, and was blowing furiously into it. The buzzing, humming toot-toot tune was loud and exciting, and people in the crowd began to clap along.

Of course, the Hot-Choc Dancers loved this. They didn't need to be asked twice and wanted to show off even more, until, that is, Grandpa Jock started to kick his legs along to the music. One of his big boots flew up, and two of the dancers fell flat on their bottoms, tripping over Grandpa Jock's huge clod-hopper feet. The security guards stepped forward to help the dancers up, and Allison knew this was her chance. She slipped in behind the guards and swiftly entered the shop. Allison was now on the inside.

She expertly dodged the second set of sliding doors, and approached Tarquin Lucius-Superbus, who was standing in the corner next to a collection of TV cameras and giant, fluffy microphones. He had been expecting her.

'Right, young lady. That old sweetheart, Mr Jock, says you need to be in this advert,' sang Tarquin with a flourish. 'And I have the powers of persuasion to make it happen. Come with me.' He turned on his heels smartly, walked beyond the dancers who had finally made it into the foyer, and marched up to the All-Days store manager, who was inspecting a gleaming basket of cauliflowers.

'If it isn't the wonderful Mr Spender,' gushed Tarquin. 'You are going to be marvellous, dear boy, marvellous. And your handsome young man too.' The director waved his hands over towards Jude, who was leaning against the vegetable shelves, now bored of shouting at staff members.

'However, in the interests of social equality, I think our advert needs the feminine touch,' Tarquin's eyes twinkled, as he presented Allison with aplomb. 'This young lady would show off the store's appeal to a whole new sector of shoppers.' Tarquin was sure that he had Grimley eating out of the palm of his hand. Jude just growled.

Grimley turned slightly to glance at his son, then launched into a volley of wild words and eye-poppingly painful threats.

'IF YOU DON'T THINK THAT ME AND MY BOY ARE GOOD ENOUGH TO STAR IN THIS ADVERT THEN I WILL SHOVE THAT CAMERA AND YOUR FLUFFY MICROPHONE RIGHT UP WHERE THE SUN DON'T SHINE!' Grimley didn't even stop for breath. 'THERE ARE ENOUGH GIRLY DANCERS IN THAT HOT-CHOC GROUP THING THAT WE DON'T NEED ANY MORE WANNABE ACTRESSES GETTING IN OUR WAY!'

Tarquin was shocked but Grimley didn't wait for a reply, instead whirling Allison around and marching her to the front doors. The security guards held the doors back, and if Grimley Spender thought he could've gotten away with it, he would've kicked Allison right up the bottom and out of his shop. But there was a big crowd out there, and some people had their mobile phones and cameras out, so Grimley just threw Allison outside, shouting,

'AND NO MORE SHOPLIFTING FROM YOU, MY GIRL!'

Allison was red-faced and shaking, trying not to look anyone in the eye. Their plan had failed at the first hurdle, and she was furious, and gutted, and embarrassed all at the same time.

What she didn't see was a strange lady walking into the shop behind her. The lady was older, and wore a dirty, beige raincoat. She had blue curlers in her white hair and she might've put her make-up on in the dark, as it was smudged all over her face. Her legs were also wet from the knees down with dirty, muddy canal water.

Allison did hear her voice however, shouting at the store manager, on the verge of tears. 'I need to come into this shop. I am expected.'

'Madam, we are very busy here today, and we don't need a bag-lady like you interrupting our advert,' snapped Grimley, trying not to raise his voice again. 'Now, push off!'

Grimley Spender turned swiftly and walked back inside his shop. The security guards stepped back, and the sliding doors slammed shut in the lady's face.

'But I'm the props lady,' she said softly to no one in particular.

Beyond the glass doors, inside the store, Allison could see Jude giggling nastily.

I WAS RAGING...

No, raging is too small a word for the way I was feeling at that moment. I was livid! Okay, I know 'livid' is actually a smaller word than 'raging' but maybe I was totally livid.

And fuming! Actually seething! And furious too! It was all of the above, rolled up into a big ball of steaming anger at being thrown out of the shop in front of all those people by that little squirt. How dare he?!

There's probably still steam coming out of my ears even now. I wanted to scream until my lungs exploded. How dare he lie to all those people! I've never stolen a thing in my life, and who would all those people believe... me, a kid or that little monster, with his suit and his briefcase and his 'I'm better than you kids' attitude, just because he's all grown up???

Grown-ups don't know everything... most of the time it's just their opinion. They think they're right all the time like 'too much chocolate's not good for you' or 'playing videos is bad for you'. My mum says reading a book in the dark with a torch is bad for your eyes (it isn't).

Some grown-ups go off and drink wine and smoke cigarettes... I've seen that Mr Spender guy smoking behind his shop. It's dis-gusting. That's why his breath stink! Some grown-ups drive too fast, and fiddle with their mobiles whilst they're driving. Either they're lying to themselves or they just don't care.

See, bullies aren't just in schools... Bullies can be adults with nice job titles, in suits and ties, who think they have the right to break the spirit of others so they can feel better about their own miserable lives. You might try to change me, Spender... but you'll never break me!

Breath, Allison. Remember... deep breaths)

And the way he spoke to that woman too... calling her a bag-lady like that. She was Tarquin's props lady for the advert. Mr Jock spoke to her, and apparently she nearly hit a runaway shopping trolley as she was driving to the superstore. Her little red car ended up in the canal, and she had to wade out of the water. Luckily it wasn't too deep.

Anyway, Mr Jock helped push her car out of the canal... and he didn't even mind getting his feet wet. He's such a kind old man! And Tarquin told Spender about how he shouted at the props lady and she couldn't get into the shop, and Tarquin was going to cancel the advert but Spender panicked and told the security guards to let the lady in the beige raincoat and blue curlers in her hair into the shop as soon as she came back.

SO THEY DID!

Chapter Twenty Five - Popped Up

The security guards exchanged glances when the props lady eventually showed up but they just shrugged their shoulders, and thought *orders are orders*, and they let her into the shop. She seemed to be an incredibly hairy woman.

She was carrying a large picnic basket filled with bread, rolls, crackers, lots of chocolate spread and strange little plastic boxes with sloppy brown gloop in them. Basically, any props she thought she might need for the advert. She was the expert, and didn't think that anyone would question her.

She was still wearing her beige raincoat, which now seemed to be a little tight for her. She still had the blue curlers in her ginger hair, and her make up was still terrible. The lower part of her legs were dry now but still dirty from the canal. Sadly, her shoes must've been ruined by the water because she'd swapped them for a pair of large boots.

'Okay, Mr Spender, darling,' chirped Tarquin, happily. 'I am being paid by the chocolate spread people to promote their new product, as well as by All-Days to advertise their fancy new shop. I am the director, and I would like you to take directions from me.'

Both Grimley Spender and Jude growled at this but kept their heads down, afraid their advert might be cancelled, and they would miss their moment of fame.

'When I say *Action* and we snap this clapper board, the wonderful Hot-Choc Dancers will do their groovy thing for the first few seconds, then you both say your lines to the camera and take a beautiful big bite of the chocolate spread. You savour it and smile to the camera. Have we all got that? Wonderful!' Tarquin beamed.

'Alright, everyone,' Tarquin clapped his hands. 'Places for full dress rehearsal please.'

The dancers moved into their opening positions, clad in their chocolate brown leotards. Hair done, and make-up immaculate.

Slowly, Jude put his hand up in the air. Grimley Spender tried to stand on his son's toes but Jude ignored him.

'Excuse me, Mr Lucius-Bus-Stop, sir,' said Jude. Grimley rolled his eyes at the very thought of such a ridiculous name.

Tarquin just rolled his eyes too. 'It's *Superbus* but never mind. Carry on, young man.'

'What if we get something wrong, or forget our lines or something?' he asked nervously. It would've been ever-so-delicious had George, Allison and Kenny been there to see the bully looking far less confident than usual but Tarquin would remember to tell them later. Somebody else might want to tell them too.

'Don't you worry about a thing, young man.' Tarquin's voice lilted merrily, as he waved his hands around, as if conducting an invisible orchestra. 'We have state-of-the-art technology here, a multi-camera set-up and a real-time digital editing system. There's a 10-second delay between live recording and the broadcast, just in case of any mishaps. When we go live, I will edit the screenshots between you, the dancers or the product, and the sound system can play the chocolate jingle at any stage. The broadcast will look slick, seamless and utterly fabulous.'

Jude seemed satisfied with this, and returned to his spot. The dancers took their positions throughout the fruit and veg section, ready for their cue. There was a huge television screen to Tarquin's left, showing the picture that each camera was picking up at that moment.

'And props into position please,' sang Tarquin with a smile, and the props lady ran across to the **Spr3d the Chocolate** display with a plate, her blue curlers bobbing beneath her thin net scarf, and she laid the dish down next to Jude and Grimley. The props lady had chosen to cover the chocolate over a selection of crispy crackers, and the brown spread gleamed beautifully underneath the spotlights.

Then the props lady slipped quietly beneath one of those spotlights and was gone. Well, as quietly as any lady could slip wearing those big clod-hopping boots.

'Ready for first rehearsal,' announced Tarquin. 'And … roll cameras!'

The cameras panned in on each of their chosen positions, as Tarquin talked through each of the shots.

'Actors looking good…' he nodded. 'Product spectacular. Dancers ready to burst into life, darlings, good, good. Fruit and veg displays immaculate. Cauliflowers looking super, all creamy white, fresh and tasty. And … in three, two, one, ACTION!'

The perky rhythm of the music kicked in and the Hot-Choc dancers leapt into action, legs flying and arms waving, as they belted out their new, catchy product jingle…

"Spr3d the Chocolate, Spr3d the Chocolate, Spr3d the Chocolate, Spr3d the Chocolate," they all sang in perfect harmony.

"Spread it on your crackers," chanted one young lady, wiggling her eye-brows up and down.

"Spread it on your bread," sang the chap with the perfect teeth and the blond, floppy hair.

"Spread it on your sandwich," smiled another girl, suspiciously happy for a chocolate spread.

"Or on your toast instead!" chirped the last guy, as he winked straight into the camera.

"Spr3d!" yelled everybody together, as they all leapt Into a frantic star jump.

One of the cameras cut to the gleaming mountain of

jars on the display, before panning backwards to squeeze Jude and Grimley into the shot. The background music was still pounding, and the two would-be actors appeared wooden, and slightly startled. Both of them were holding a chocolate-covered cracker in their right hand.

Behind the cameras, Tarquin rolled his hands together, as if telling his actors to keep it going before Grimley remembered his one and only line.

'I've - I've spread my chocolate,' he stammered into camera two.

'And I've spread mine!' Jude beamed, taking a huge bite from his crunchy cracker. The chocolate spread was certainly delicious, thick and creamy with a hint of hazelnuts.

"*Spr3d!*" The dancers crowded around the two actors, waving their jazz hands in celebration, and twinkling their all-too-perfect smiles.

'And CUT!' yelled Tarquin, clapping his hands, and walking out from behind his monitor. 'Dancers, you were wonderful. Very sharp on your mark, young man. Jude, you've taken a bad line and made it better. Little bit quicker with your delivery, Grimley, but you had me hooked. I really did believe you had spread your own chocolate.'

Beside the display, the plate of crackers was almost empty. Each of the dancers had swooped in and snatched up a biscuit but Jude had scoffed the rest himself. Grimley had finished off the cracker in his hand, and the sweet, sticky chocolate had clagged around his lips. He wiped his mouth with the back of his hand, and snarled. Being the star of his own advert wasn't as easy as he first imagined, and he wasn't enjoying himself. He didn't feel in control.

Tarquin danced between the cameras, the monitor, the actors and the set, shouting instructions in a positive, delightful way, and everybody responded with zeal. There was an energy on the set, and the dancers and the crew were buzzing.

'Alright, you lovely people,' Tarquin crooned. 'Reset on the monitors, actors ready, dancers take your positions for the final rehearsal. Props, can we have more crackers, please.'

And the props lady delivered another plate of chocolate crackers to the set.

'Marvellous, darlings, marvellous,' gushed Tarquin, with such gusto that even Grimley felt a wave of relief wash over him. His shoulders relaxed, and for the first time since the filming started, he felt confident.

Jude, on the other hand, was feeling slightly queasy, since he had finished the last plate of crackers all to himself. The dancers had declined the snacks this time because they said they were all watching their figures, and Jude thought it would be rude not to eat them. Not that Jude was ever worried about being rude.

Tarquin went on again. 'Three minutes to the live broadcast, you superstars! There will be ten million people watching around the globe, on their TVs, their laptops and their phones but don't let that worry you.' Grimley gulped. Jude just smiled.

A small man, with the biggest headset ever made, ran around the front of the monitors and tugged at Tarquin's arm. He pulled the little microphone up close to his mouth and whispered into it. Tarquin pressed one of the ear-pieces on his headset closer and listened carefully. Then he nodded.

'Props! Props, love,' yelled Tarquin, snapping his fingers. The props lady leapt up from the darkness behind the checkout counter. Tarquin spoke to her loudly, 'The sound engineer tells me that the crackers are making too much noise, crunching into the actors' microphones. We need something a little quieter for the live action shot.'

Tarquin bowed his head, as the props lady whispered in his ear, (she wasn't important enough to deserve a big pair of headsets). The director turned and boomed back to the set, 'Actors, darlings ... we've cut out the crackers and will be going with the sandwiches. Just give me the same wonderful flourish when you bite into them, thank you. Two minutes to show time, people!'

TWO MINUTES?! At this, the props lady sprinted off behind the monitors towards her picnic basket, and there followed an odd banging and clattering of plastic boxes and containers. The sound engineer was certain that one of the microphones had picked up a faint *Shizzle Sticks!* but he hadn't pressed record yet, so he couldn't check it back.

The new sandwiches were swiftly delivered to the set before Tarquin could yell '*One minute!*' and the props lady had retreated back behind the monitors, out of sight. The two slices of bread were soft and white, and the layer of chocolate spread was thick and gooey in the middle. But Jude frowned, and looked puzzled.

'Dad?' he said quietly. 'Did you think the props lady had a moustache, Dad? A big ginger one?'

'Shut up, boy,' hissed Grimley. 'We're about to go live,' as he tightened the knot on his tie nervously.

Tarquin now snapped his fingers, and another technician jumped out with a black and white clapperboard. 'Quiet on the set please,' he yelled. 'And ... in five, four, three.' The two and the one were silent but the clapperboard guy signalled them with his fingers, then pointed to the dancers with a sweeping arm.

The beat pounded in and the dancers were off, skipping, prancing and jazzing their way up the fruit and veg aisle, singing,

"Spr3d the Chocolate. Spr3d the Chocolate. Spr3d the Chocolate. Spr3d the Chocolate,"
"Spread it on your crackers,"
"Spread it on your bread,"
"Spread it on your sandwich,"
"Or on your toast instead!"
"Spr3d!" and the camera cut to Grimley and Jude, standing together smiling.

'I've spread my chocolate,' beamed Grimley, with a twinkle in his eye.

'And I've spread mine!' Jude declared , taking a huge bite from his sandwich, and he swallowed a large mouthful of chocolate, trying to look very pleased with himself. Grimley Spender timed it perfectly, so that he too took a bite from his sandwich.

"Spr3d!" The dancers sang, as they crowded around the two stars, and the cameras zoomed in to capture the final shot. Jude and Grimley choked and stared at each other. Their sandwiches flopped, as the bread drooped into a limp, soggy mess in their hands. Chocolate spread dripped out through their fingers and down the front of their sparklingly white shirts.

As the taste spread around their mouths, Jude and Grimley suddenly realised that the filling on their sandwiches wasn't chocolate spread at all.

It was disgusting. In fact, it was so disgusting, it tasted like poo. Now, it was Jude's turn to barf.

'Bleeeeeeeeeeuuuuuuuuggggggggggggghhhhhhhh!

An enormous bolt of projectile vomit sprayed from his mouth and splattered over the lens of camera one. Clumps of cracker and brown goo dripped slowly down the screen.

'Switch to camera two,' yelled Tarquin, as the dancers shuffled back out of shot, and away from the two actors.

It was now Grimley's turn to eject his stomach contents. The taste in his mouth was sharp, bitter and acidic, a burning, sickly yak that churned his stomach and sent the first portion of puke flying over the jars of chocolate spread on the display stand. The stench was over-powering, and Jude, who had been catching his breath between pukes and dribbling on the floor, took his turn to spew again. This time, Jude's vomit hit the sound engineer who was trying to hide behind a large microphone.

Then Grimley Spender spewed on the cauliflowers.

Jude barfed on the shopping baskets at the door.

Grimley looked left, then right, then just puked over the floor, and as the Hot-Choc dancers jumped back in disgust, some of them were slipping and sliding in the mess. The scene was chaos but surprisingly, no one had heard Tarquin shout 'CUT!' yet.

Because he hadn't, because he was still filming, cutting each shot and editing the digital footage just before it was broadcast to the world. Millions and millions of people were watching Jude and Grimley throw up all over the All-Days store. It certainly wasn't a good advert for Spr3d either, especially with all the sound effects that Jude and Grimley were hacking, coughing and gobbing into the microphones.

Finally, Grimley's stomach was empty, and he fought to get his breath back.

'That was poo,' he gasped. 'That wasn't chocolate. That was poop. Somebody fed us a poo sandwich!' He straightened up, ignoring his son, who was still barfing behind the chocolate spread jars. Some of the camera team were hiding their laughter behind their hands but, as professionals, they kept filming. It was the director's job to say when they should stop.

'Where's that props lady? She did it,' he screeched, the burning flavour still catching at the back of his throat.

'She had a moustache,' wheezed Jude, weakly. He was too ill to stand up.

'We've lost the props lady,' shouted Grimley. 'Find her now,' he ordered.

'Well, you've already lost one props lady today, darling. That was just unfortunate. To lose two prop ladies is simply carelessness.' Tarquin delivered his line with a flourish.

'Where is she then, or they, or whatever?' stammered Grimley, his suit still dripping with thick gloop.

'The first lady went home, after you were very rude to her,' smiled Tarquin sweetly. 'The second lady, well, I don't think you'll ever see her again. You see, I think that was the revenge of the Soggy Sa-turd-day Sandwich.' His face was a picture of innocence.

Fuming now, and forgetting he was still being filmed, Grimley Spender stomped over to the checkout counter, reached behind it and lifted up his shiny, leather briefcase. He swung it around his head and launched himself towards Tarquin's head, but the director ducked behind his monitors.

Grimley missed and his briefcase smashed straight into camera one (the one covered in Jude's first bolt of barf). The briefcase burst open and hundreds of pieces of paper fluttered out. It was like a wedding, or a ticker-tape parade, or a celebration, as the shop was littered with notes and letters gently floating down to the ground.

Tarquin was first to his feet, snatched up a handful of paper, and walked calmly over to camera two. He lifted his head, waved the letters at the lens, and read.

'"Dear All-Days, your store manager is a disgrace" and here's another, *"To who it may concern, that new manager is evil,"* Tarquin went on reading. *"The manager, Spender I think his name is, is rude, obnoxious and nasty."*

Editor's note

Apologies again, readers. That was probably the most disgusting chapter in the history of children's literature. However, I need to point out that, as a grown-up, I have read another book called The Help by Kathryn Stockett. It's an adult book, and if your teacher is giggling right now, she or he has probably read it. That book has won loads of prizes, and it's been turned into a movie, yet it features a character who bakes a poop pie and gives it to her boss, who then eats it!

So it's not just yucky children's authors who write disgusting stuff.

Chapter Twenty Seven - Popped In

Grimley pushed his way into the screenshot, shoving Tarquin out in the process. Turning to the camera, he blabbered...

'No, no, no, it's all a mistake,' Grimley sneered. 'These aren't real customer complaints. They're just jokes, meant to be funny. My customers love me really.'

Right behind camera two, there was a commotion going on. The sliding doors had been pushed wide open and three children were charging towards Grimley Spender. The security guards were too busy on their phones chuckling, with tears running down their cheeks, and the crowd outside were also red-faced and laughing.

George pulled at Kenny's sleeve and held him back, as Allison marched right up to Grimley. She stared him right in the face, took a deep breath and let loose her frustrations.

'Mr Spender, you are a horrible little man! And your customers don't like you. In fact, they are not *your* customers, they are just people who need to shop here because this big superstore has closed the real greengrocers, and the butchers and the bakers in the town. All the little shops. It's just greed.'

Allison paused for breath and camera two moved around and zoomed into her face. 'You only care about yourself,' she went on. 'You have no friends. Your son, Jude, has no friends, and he takes that from you. I'm lucky, I have two very good friends, who would do anything to help me. They might be a bit silly sometimes, one of them can be disgusting but their hearts are in the right place. You, sir, have lost your heart, if you ever had one!'

Grimley was shrinking away from Allison's volley of anger. She was right, and he knew it. His fragile, protective shell of arrogance was crumbling beneath Allison's words. The truth hurts.

'I hope this is the end for you because there are better ways of speaking to people, just look at Tarquin.' Allison nodded across to the director. 'But this is not the end for us, for me and George and Kenny. You see, in my ending, Endeavour Never Dies and our Energy Never Dies. You, sir, are an energy vampire, sucking the life out of those who don't want to shout as loudly or as rudely as you!'

Tarquin, the dancers, the camera team and the technicians burst into a spontaneous round of applause, and, although Allison's face had turned red, she took a small bow.

On the other hand, Grimley Spender's face was a pale, sickly yellow shade, and Allison had just shown the world his true colours. He turned around swiftly, and desperate to escape the camera's glare, he ran up the fruit and veg aisle towards the warehouse, leaving Jude hobbling along behind him, feebly croaking, 'Dad, wait for me, Dad!'

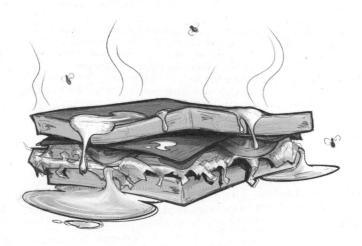

SEE, I TOLD YOU I WAS RAGING...

ANGRY FIST →

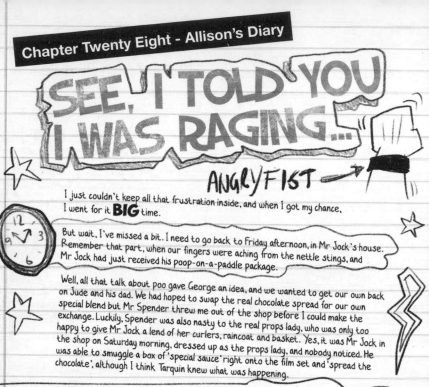

I just couldn't keep all that frustration inside, and when I got my chance, I went for it **BIG** time.

But wait, I've missed a bit. I need to go back to Friday afternoon, in Mr Jock's house. Remember that part, when our fingers were aching from the nettle stings, and Mr Jock had just received his poop-on-a-paddle package.

Well, all that talk about poo gave George an idea, and we wanted to get our own back on Jude and his dad. We had hoped to swap the real chocolate spread for our own special blend but Mr Spender threw me out of the shop before I could make the exchange. Luckily, Spender was also nasty to the real props lady, who was only too happy to give Mr Jock a lend of her curlers, raincoat and basket. Yes, it was Mr Jock in the shop on Saturday morning, dressed up as the props lady, and nobody noticed. He was able to smuggle a box of 'special sauce' right onto the film set and 'spread the chocolate', although I think Tarquin knew what was happening.

The first two servings on the crackers were real chocolate spread but the third, on the soggy bread, was our secret recipe. No, it wasn't real poo! That would be waaaaay too disgusting. Mr Jock had gathered together a bunch of stuff from his cupboards, his shed and the pond at the bottom of his garden. We took turns at mixing together raw onion, frog spawn (from the pond), worms, turmeric, cocoa powder (for colour), raw garlic, lemon juice and some mouldy cheese that we found at the back of Mr Jock's fridge. Kenny suggested we add haggis, because he'd heard that was pretty disgusting but Mr Jock clipped him playfully around the ear at that point. Kenny just giggled.

Mr Jock also took some fish out of his freezer, and mashed into a paste with the other stuff. Our special recipe was going to be left out in the warm air all night, so we knew this was going to taste funky in the morning.
Then, to finish it off, George wanted to wipe in some of his earwax. Kenny picked his nose, and added a few boogers, whilst Mr Jock took off his socks and scraped bits of skin from between his toes. Human parmesan cheese, he called it.
Once that was all mixed together, the smell was overpowering, so Mr Jock sprayed it with air freshener and added another sprinkle of cocoa powder.
At first, it felt wrong. But when Mr Spender called me a shoplifter and threw me out of the shop, I knew there was no going back.

#NoRegrets

Chapter Twenty Nine - Monday At School

Lunchtime, and it was the last week of school before the summer holidays. The three amigos gathered by the hole in the fence at the bottom of the playground, and Kenny was recreating the good old times by pushing, then pulling his head in and out between the extended gap in the bars, grinning as he did so.

This is the first time the children had had a chance to catch up properly since Saturday's adventures, and nobody knew quite where to begin. George and Allison just stared at each with their eyes agog, shaking their heads.

Kenny interrupted their silence. 'You'll never guess what my little brother Johnny's latest question was this morning?' Without waiting for an answer, Kenny went on. 'We were just sitting there at the breakfast table, and the little nutter asks "What would you rather eat, Kenny? Poo-flavoured chocolate or chocolate flavoured poo." Well, mum went mental, especially after his chocolate binge on Saturday morning.'

'I guess he's feeling better now,' laughed George. 'I mean, after *Barf-Gate*.'

George smiled and stuck his tongue out with a *bleugh* motion. By now, everybody had seen little Johnny's bout of sickness all over the cauliflowers, and everybody was calling it *Barf-Gate*. The camera crew had been setting up their equipment, and caught Johnny's barf, and Grimley Spender's rant to Glen about washing the puke-covered cauliflowers, during one of the test-runs of the cameras. The tide of customer disgust had been turning against All-Days and their *Barf-Gate* episode all weekend.

'Yeah, much better, thanks. There's not much can keep the wee man down for long,' smiled Kenny, proud that his little brother had puked in front of the TV cameras. Although it hadn't gone out live, half a million had already watched it on YouTube.

'And nobody keeps you down for long either, Allison, Eh?' George nodded and his eyebrows danced. Allison just shuffled her feet together.

'Yeah, you were in full flow, girl,' cried Kenny, equally proud of Allison's performance during the adverts. TV companies had refused to go back to their regular programs, and kept Allison's live rant going, and their switchboards were jammed with people calling in to praise that *brave, young girl*, they said.

'It was nothing really,' smiled Allison, bashfully. 'I just don't want people to think they can mess with me.'

'Wow,' gasped George. 'There's nobody gonna mess with you now, Allison. You were brilliant!'

'Erm, talking of mess,' said Kenny. 'You'll have noticed that Jude isn't in school today.'

Jude's desk had been empty all morning. The last anybody had seen of him, and Grimley Spender too for that matter, was when they disappeared behind the plastic curtains into the warehouse on Saturday morning. They hadn't been seen since.

George knew that Grandpa Jock had been up to their house to hand his notice in, he'd decided to quit the supermarket, and was looking forward to telling Grimley to his face. He said he'd been inspired by Allison on the TV but their house was empty and in darkness. Grandpa Jock had rung their doorbell, even banged on their door but there was no one at home. Unless Jude and Grimley were hiding behind the sofa in disgrace.

Allison nodded. 'I don't think we'll see them again, to be honest. School holidays start next week, so Jude will stay off until then. And after the summer, he's supposed to go to the secondary school but who knows.'

'And my Grandpa Jock says that Grimley Spender will be fired by All-Days for hiding all those customer complaints,' George added.

'Not to mention that disaster of an advert,' laughed Kenny. 'The way Jude sprayed that first camera with his puke … *rocket-esque*, like.' Kenny fanned his fingers out in a splatting motion, whilst he blew a raspberry with his tongue.

'At least Tarquin got paid too, from both companies. Blamed Grimley for ruining the advert,' said George. 'He reckons he'll win an award for his short *fly-on-the-wall* drama.'

'AWARD!' yelled George, slapping his hand to his forehead. 'Miss Mack said there was a prize for the best fable but I forgot to write anything. We'll be in big trouble!'

'Ah yeah, me too,' groaned Kenny. 'Wait, we can just pretend our *nettle-esque* hands were too sore to write.' And he winked at George. 'Don't suppose you wrote anything either, Allison?'

She thought for a moment.

In truth, Allison had spent the rest of the weekend writing up her fable, and lots of other thoughts in her diary. She wanted to title it *Her Story*, not history, not *his story* because the tale was about her but it didn't sound *fable-esque* enough.

Her Story was about a humble princess who felt frustrated and over-shadowed by her two older, yet idiotic, brothers. Without their father's permission, the two princes had gone off on a quest looking for adventure but had been captured by a loud, angry Ogre and his wicked dwarf. Long ago, the Ogre had stolen a powerful wand from an old wizard, and had been casting spells over the King's land ever since.

And because they hadn't asked for his permission, the king refused to rescue the two princes, leaving them trapped in the ogre's dungeon. The princess knew that her brothers were often foolhardy but their hearts were in the right place, so she decided to *grasp the nettle*.

The princess rode off on her mighty steed, a fine and

noble horse called Tarquin, until she found the Ogre's lair. The princess was able to steal the wand, and with it she'd found her own magic power, and defeated both the Ogre and the dwarf, banishing them from her kingdom.

The two princes were grateful for being rescued, the older prince gifting the princess ten fields of wheat and cereal, and his favourite tavern in the village. The younger boy had little to offer but promised to watch over her whenever she slept.

Allison shook herself out of her thoughts, and said, 'No, I didn't finish my story either. I'll speak to Miss Mack about our hands, and I'm sure we can get another couple of days to finish them. We can hand our stories in together.'

'Brilliant!' shouted the boys together. 'You're the best, Allison,' added George.

'I'm gonna put more snot zombies in my fable,' laughed Kenny. 'And you can be one of them.'

Allison laughed too, and grabbed both boys by their necks, stretching her arms around them in a big bear hug, and pulling them in closer.

'C'mere you muppets,' she yelled. 'GROUP HUG!!!!' And she wrestled with the two boys, as they tried to get away.

'No, gross!' cried George. 'I can't hug a girl. Someone might be watching.'

'I'll catch girl cooties! GIRL COOTIES!' squealed Kenny, wriggling to get away. 'Urgh! And no kissing. My teeth will fall out again!'

'Maybe I'll rescue you two muppets one day,' she said, finally letting them go.

Allison laughed at the thought that, looking forward, at some point, maybe her two friends wouldn't mind giving her a big hug one day. That's what friends do.

What's the worst that could happen?

Chapter Thirty - Finale

Author's note

I was going to call this the Epilogue but not any more. Not after all those cheeky Prologue comments. So na-na-na-na-na

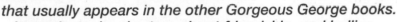

So, there we have it. A lovely, Gorgeous George story, with no aliens, no Loch Ness monsters and certainly no snot zombies, if you ignore little Johnny's runny nose in Chapter Thirteen. There was no time travelling, and none of the far-fetched nonsense that usually appears in the other Gorgeous George books.

It was just a lovely story about friendship, and bullies, and laughing at people covered in poo. Then people eating poo, or at least, thinking they'd eaten poo.

Actually, there was a lot of barfing too, wasn't there? Maybe it wasn't all that nice after all. Maybe this story even made some people feel sick, if I'm honest. Sorry.

Hold on, no, I'm not sorry. It made me laugh when I was writing it, and hopefully, if it made you laugh too, then that's all that matters. The world needs more laughter.

And talking of laughter, one thing that needs to be

pointed out here is the name of TV director Tarquin Lucius-Superbus. That's not a made-up name... seriously! It's a real name!

The Latin name in full is actually Lucius Tarquinius Superbus and refers to the seventh and final King of Rome, accepted by scholars as a real historical figure. He died in 495bc, and he was a bit of a bully, having a lot of senators put to death during his reign. The Superbus *part of his name means* the proud. *The name* Tarquin Lucius-Superbus *just made me laugh.*

However, the next Gorgeous George *book will be yucky, very yucky, perhaps even yuckier than this one... Grandpa Jock mentioned that he'd been chasing vampires in Transylvania in Chapter Twenty, so we might have to explore that story a bit further.*

I was going to call it Grandpa Jock and the Vampire's Veggie Vomit *because there's always carrots and sweetcorn in the puke puddle when you're sick. But having a disgusting word like* vomit *in the title might put readers off. There are only two times when* vomit *is not disgusting. First, when you have a funny little emoji like this:*

And second, when vomit *is followed by the word* comet, *like being on a super-fast roller-coaster that leaves your tummy at the top of the hill and it doesn't catch up until you reach the end.*

There's even an aeroplane ride called The Vomit Comet *that goes up and down at rocket speeds on the edge of the earth's atmosphere. For a few seconds your body is weightless, and you're floating in zero-gravity, then next moment, you and your stomach are plunged back down to earth. It only costs about five thousand pounds (yes, £5,000!) so there are plenty of cheaper ways to feel queasy.*

So, not the Vampire's Veggie Vomit *then. What about* Vlad's Vampire Veggies? *About a mad scientist in*

Transylvania who creates blood-sucking vegetables in his laboratory, and when he brings them to life with lightning and electricity, he shouts "IT'S ALIVE! It's alive!" in a weird, overly-dramatic fashion. And that would be pretty cool because we won't have colour pages in the next book (except the cover), so the black and white images would look dark, stylish and mysterious.

That's it! Next book idea sorted! Sorry I can't tell you any more ... it's top secret. You'll just have to buy a copy when it comes out. Or ask your headteacher to invite me back to your school!

Things to do at home or in the class.

- Google the meaning of your name.

- Write a short story using your name and an alliterative title.

- Keep a diary and write your thoughts in it every day for a week.

- Form a comb and paper band and play your favourite tunes.

- Play the prune and spoon race.

- Create your own -*esque* type words and use them in the correct context.

- Read some of Aesop's fables.

- Write your own fables with a positive message.

- Can you write a -*Gate* episode that has happened in your school? Something like *Teacher-Gate*, or *Bench-Gate*, or *Hamster-Gate* (if your class is allowed to keep hamsters as a pet).

- What is your name spelled backwards?

- What's the wackiest, funniest character's name you can come up with?

- Invent new products to sell, like hob-bobs and Spr3d the chocolate, and create an advertising campaign and slogan.

The Very First Gorgeous George Audio Book

Have you ever read an audio book? Well, no, of course not because you don't read an audio book, you listen to them. The clue is in the title.

Well, the 8th adventure in the Gorgeous George series, Grandpa Jock and the Incredible Iron-Bru-Man Incident has been turned into our first audio book!

This book has been awarded **5 Stars - Highly Recommended - FINALIST** prize at the **Wishing Shelf Book Awards 2022!**

Star Rating: ☆☆☆☆☆
Narrator Performance: 9/10
Writing Style: 8/10
Content/Plot: 8/10
Cover: 5/5
Sound Quality/Music/
Sound Effects: 4/5

Available on Amazon and Amazon Audible
- **100%** of listeners would listen to another book by this author.
- **100%** of listeners would listen to another book narrated by this performer.
- **100%** of listeners thought the cover was good or excellent.
- **100%** of listeners felt it was easy to follow.
- **100%** of listeners would recommend this audiobook to another listener to try.

Some Listeners' Comments

"This is a very funny story. I liked the narrator who had a Scottish accent and sounded like Scotty in Star Trek." Boy listener, aged 14

"The narrator sounded like Scotty from Star Trek"

"I thought this was a comical story with lots of cool words like Swizzle Sticks – which I probably spelt wrong. I liked the idea of a grandad being a super-hero. Also, I liked that it was never boring and was often very exciting. The beginning is amazingly exciting!" Boy, aged 14

"This is a funny sort of book. I liked the characters, particularly Grandpa Jock. And the kid characters were cool too, although I did get them a bit mixed up. I thought the writer did an AMAZING job of writing a funny, exciting story, and the narrator who told the story made it exciting too. I would read lots of books by this author." Girl, aged 13

To Sum It Up:

'A fast-paced, super-fun adventure for kids.
A FINALIST and highly recommended!'

Available on Amazon and Amazon Audible

About the author, Stuart Reid

At the time of printing, Stuart Reid is 55 years old, going on 10. He's just a big kid really but by the time you've read this he's probably much, much older.

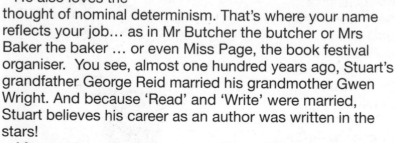

He thinks it is incredibly funny when his name Stuart Reid is spelt backwards it makes Dier Trauts which sounds like a rather nasty stomach infection.

He also loves the thought of nominal determinism. That's where your name reflects your job... as in Mr Butcher the butcher or Mrs Baker the baker ... or even Miss Page, the book festival organiser. You see, almost one hundred years ago, Stuart's grandfather George Reid married his grandmother Gwen Wright. And because 'Read' and 'Write' were married, Stuart believes his career as an author was written in the stars!

After turning up at the wrong college, Stuart was forced to spend the next 25 years being boring, professional and corporate. He is allergic to ties; blaming them for stifling the blood flow to his imagination, and his fun-loving attitude was further crushed by the weight of career responsibility, as a business manager in the retail and hospitality industries in the UK and Middle East. One day, he decided to give it all up to become a writer.

Stuart is one of the busiest authors in the world today, performing at schools, libraries and book festivals with his book events, Reading Rocks! He has appeared at over 2,500 schools since 2011, throughout Britain, Ireland, India, Abu Dhabi, Dubai, Hong Kong and Australia.

He won the Forward National Literature Silver Seal in 2012 for his debut novel, *Gorgeous George and the Giant Geriatric Generator*. Stuart's 7th book *Gorgeous George and the Timewarp Trouser Trumpets* won the silver medal at the Wishing Shelf Book Awards, whilst his 8th title *Grandpa Jock and the Incredible Iron-Bru-Man Incident* was launched at TalkSport Radio on the Hawksbee and Jacobs Show to an audience of over three million listeners.

He has also been presented with an Enterprise in Education Champion Award from Falkirk Council.

Stuart has been married to Audrey for over thirty years. He has two children, Jess and Charley, a spiky haircut and an awesome man-cave filled with cool stuff!

About the illustrator, John Pender

John is 43 and currently lives in Grangemouth with his wife Angela and their young son, Lucas, aged 11.

John has been a professional Art Director and illustrator since he was 18 years old, contracted to create illustrations, artwork and digital logos for businesses around the world, along with a host of individual commissions of varying degrees.

Being a comic book lover since the age of 4, illustration is his true passion, doodling everything from the likes of Transformers, to Danger Mouse to anything Marvel and DC-related in pursuit of honing his skills over the years.

As well as cartoon and comic book art, John is also an accomplished traditional and digital artist, specialising in a more realistic form of art for this medium, and draws his

inspiration from acclaimed names such as Charlie Adlard, famous for The Walking Dead graphic novels, Brett Parson of Tank Girl fame, as well as the renowned Joe Madureira, Leinil Yu, Steve McNiven and Gary Frank.

John has been married to Angela for 11 years and he describes his wife as his 'source of inspiration, positivity and motivation for life.' John enjoys the relaxation and stress-relief that family life can bring.